WAR WORK

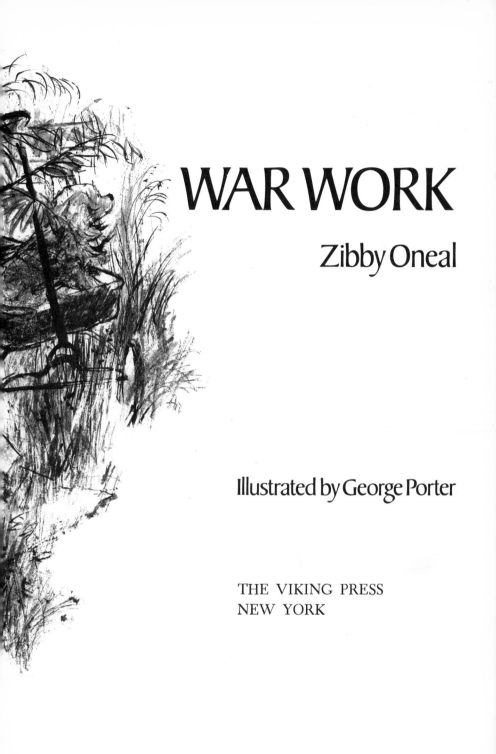

WAR WORK

Zibby Oneal

Illustrated by George Porter

THE VIKING PRESS
NEW YORK

FIRST PUBLISHED IN 1971 BY THE VIKING PRESS, INC.
625 MADISON AVENUE, NEW YORK, N.Y. 10022
PUBLISHED SIMULTANEOUSLY IN CANADA BY
THE MACMILLAN COMPANY OF CANADA LIMITED

LIBRARY OF CONGRESS CATALOG CARD NUMBER: 77–162673

FIC 1. WORLD WAR II   670–75000–X   VLB 670–75001–8

PRINTED IN U.S.A.   1   2   3   4   5   75   74   73   72   71

FOR LISA AND MICHAEL

WAR WORK

(1)

Rosie, and Zoe sat on their front porch swatting mosquitoes. "This is the worst summer of my entire life," Zoe said.

"Me too," said Rosie.

Zoe looked at her sister. "Do you ever have any ideas of your own?" she asked.

Rosie scratched a mosquito bite and said nothing. "You're a dumb copycat, Rosie."

Rosie stood up. She smoothed out the wrinkles in her shorts. She looked slowly up and down the street. Then she bent over and with the tip ends of her fingernails gave Zoe a hard pinch on the leg.

"Ouch!" Zoe jumped up. She doubled her fist and aimed a punch at Rosie. "You dumb baby!" she screamed. "You stupid copycat!"

Rosie had moved out of the way. She stood quietly smiling, looking at the screen door. "You—" Zoe yelled. She stopped. Too late, as usual, she realized what was happening. There stood her mother peering through the screen. Her glasses were pushed on top of her head and her hair was sticking up like a wire brush. Zoe remembered it was Bill Day.

"I have told you seven dozen times that when I am paying the bills I have to have quiet!" their mother said. It was true. She *had* told them seven dozen times, at least. Paying bills was hard for their mother because she counted on her fingers. "When I finish the bills I'll take you swimming," she said, "but, Zoe, if you keep interrupting it will take me all afternoon."

"But Rosie—" Zoe shouted.

"Just never mind. I don't want to hear about Rosie." Their mother settled her glasses back on her nose and disappeared into the cool gloom of the house.

"You dumb rat!" Zoe muttered under her breath. "You never get blamed for anything."

Rosie sat back down on the front steps. "Sticks and stones will break my bones," she murmured. She was crazy about sayings like that.

Zoe sat down beside her. If just once I could remember not to yell, she thought. But she knew she never would. When she was mad she yelled. She had to. It was like throwing up. You had to and you did, even in department stores.

"I wish we were in California," Rosie said. "This is the first summer of my whole life that we haven't gone to the seashore."

"Wow—eight whole summers!" said Zoe. "I've gone for ten. Anyway, we can't this year."

"Because of the War," said Rosie.

"Do tell," said Zoe.

The War was all anyone talked about. Zoe was sick of it. At dinner her father talked about troop movements and battlefields. Downtown in the stores radios broadcast War news. If ever the War was over, nobody would have anything to talk about. Zoe couldn't imagine what might be in the newspaper if the Germans weren't bombing London or the Japanese weren't invading Saipan. The Germans and the Japanese were the enemies. They were constantly doing something to make her father swear.

As far as Zoe was concerned, the war was ruining everything. It had already ruined their vacation. They couldn't take the train to California because trains were crowded with soldiers going back and forth to Army bases. Their mother said it would be unpatriotic to take train space from soldiers who needed it. They couldn't drive, either, because gasoline was rationed.

Practically everything good is rationed, Zoe thought. That meant that besides money you needed ration stamps to buy many things. Meat, butter, sugar, even shoes were scarce because of the War and you needed stamps to get them. Ration stamps came in red and blue, and Zoe's mother was always running out.

Practically none of Zoe's friends had fathers at home because of the War. They were all overseas on battlefields. Rosie's and Zoe's father wasn't. He was a doctor. He had to stay home to take care of civilians. A few other fathers had to stay home to run stores. Fathers like this were called "essential."

"I wish our father wasn't essential," Zoe said.

"Somebody has to take care of sick people," said Rosie.

That was true. If their father weren't a doctor, if he were a businessman like Opal Wheeler's father, he wouldn't be essential. Of course then he might have to go to War. That gave Zoe a funny feeling. Libby Purcell's father had gone into the Army and the Purcells had a little banner with a blue star on it hanging in their window. It meant that Libby's father was at war. Mrs. Nutt, who lived across the street, had a gold star in her window. That was because Mrs. Nutt's son had been blown up at Bataan. Bataan was a battlefield. Mrs. Nutt's son was dead.

"I hate this summer," said Rosie. "I want to swim in the ocean."

"You don't know how to swim in the ocean. You can barely swim in a pool."

Rosie scratched a mosquito bite. "There's nothing to do here," she said.

There were things to do, but nothing seemed interesting. They could play Parcheesi or paper dolls or they could go across the street and tease Mrs. Nutt's Afghan hound. They could ask their mother for something to do, but she'd probably just tell them to weed the radishes. They grew radishes, tomatoes, corn, and carrots in a patch behind the house. It was their Victory garden. Most people had Victory gardens because of the War. If you raised your own tomatoes, that left more store tomatoes for soldiers. At least that was how Zoe understood it. She knew it was patriotic to weed the garden, just as it was patriotic to save tin foil and rubber scrap and old grease. How all this helped the War was a mystery to her, though.

Zoe sat and looked first up one side of the street and then down the other. Nothing was going on. On every front lawn a sprinkler was turning, except across the street in Mrs. Padmore's yard. Mrs. Padmore was old. She just let her grass burn up in the summer.

Half the houses had green-and-white-striped awnings. Two had plain green. One had pink. The pink ones belonged to Miss Lavatier. Miss Lavatier was a spinster. If you went to her house for some reason, to collect for the Red Cross or to ask for tin foil, for instance, she never answered the door right away. You would stand waiting for a long time. Pretty soon you'd hear the Venetian blinds rattle at the living-room window and there would be one of Miss Lavatier's eyes peering at you. After all that she'd answer the door. Zoe's mother said spinsters were nervous because they lived alone. Zoe didn't think Miss Lavatier was nervous. She thought she was odd.

Anyway, Miss Lavatier never had what you wanted, no matter what it was. Joe Bunch said Miss Lavatier's house was probably completely empty. Joe Bunch also said that Miss Lavatier had a boyfriend who was a gangster, but Joe Bunch exaggerated a lot.

The Bunches lived down at the end of the block on the corner of Victoria Street. Mr. Bunch ran the Queenie Drugstore. He was a crabby man. He yelled at you if you handled the penny candy. He screamed if you read a comic from the rack and didn't buy it. If a child got on Mr. Bunch's nerves too much he called the child's mother. If that didn't work he called the police. Mr. Bunch had six children. They were all scared of him.

"Too bad Mr. Bunch is essential," Zoe said, half to herself.

"What?"

"Nothing. I wasn't talking to you."

"Here comes Joe Bunch's dog," Rosie said.

Joe Bunch's dog was named Fang. He was a fat cream-colored cocker spaniel, blind in one eye and six years old. Joe said Fang had a killer instinct, but Zoe didn't believe it. He came waddling up the sidewalk toward Rosie and Zoe, panting and looking friendly. "Hi, Fang," Zoe said. "Where's Joe?" She asked just to say something. She could already see Joe way down at the end of the street rounding the corner. He was pulling a wagon.

They watched him coming toward them. Whatever he had in the wagon was heavy. He was tugging the load along as if he were moving a house. And whatever it was sparkled.

"Maybe Joe Bunch found some diamonds," Rosie said.

Sometimes it was embarrassing to be related to Rosie.

"Do you think if it was diamonds he'd be pulling them along in plain sight where any robber or gangster could see?" Zoe asked.

"Well, I don't see any robbers around," said Rosie.

"Rosie, robbers don't stand right out in the middle of

the street with signs pinned on them saying, 'I'm a robber,' you know. They hide behind things."

"Some do. Some don't," Rosie said. Zoe felt like hitting her again.

Joe was nearing the house. He disappeared behind a bridal-wreath bush and reappeared, clattering.

"Hi, Joe!" Rosie called. She jumped off the porch steps and went running toward him. "What's in your wagon?" Zoe followed, tucking her shirt into her shorts.

"Tin cans!" Rosie said, disappointed. "I thought it would be something exciting."

"Sure, tin cans," Joe Bunch said. "It's my second load today. I'm taking them down to the armory." Everyone was saving tin cans that summer because of the War. The Army needed tin for something or other. But Joe Bunch saved more than anyone. He searched for them. Twice a week he went through all the trash cans in the neighborhood in case someone had forgotten about the War and thrown one out. Then he flattened them by stamping on them. When he had a wagonload he took it to the armory. Also, he collected old newspapers, tied them in bundles with twine, and took them to the armory. Joe Bunch's tin-foil ball was the biggest in the neighborhood. He planned to take *it* to the armory soon, but he kept putting off doing it until the ball was bigger. Nobody knew exactly what happened to all the cans and newspapers and tin foil once it reached the armory, but everyone knew it was important. Joe Bunch said they made tanks out of it.

"You have any cans you want me to take along?" Joe asked casually. Zoe knew perfectly well he wasn't trying to be helpful. He just wanted to have the biggest load of cans anybody brought to the armory that day. She could see straight through Joe Bunch but she sort of liked him anyway.

"We probably have some," Zoe said. "Wait while I look."

16

She ran up the porch steps and slammed through the screen door, remembering too late that it was Bill Day. To make up for it she tiptoed down the hall to the kitchen where Bernice, their maid, was scrubbing the floor. "Look out where you're walking," Bernice said. "The floor's all wet."

"I have to get our cans," Zoe said.

"Well, the Japanese aren't going to win the War if you wait five minutes. By then the floor will be dry."

"Can't wait," Zoe said, tiptoeing across the wet linoleum. She knew Bernice would grumble but that she wouldn't really be mad. "Anyway, my feet are clean."

"Oh, spotless," Bernice muttered, coming along behind her with the mop.

There was about half a carton of cans in the back hall. Zoe picked it up. "I'll go out the back door," she said.

"Oh, wonderful. Thank you, Your Highness," said Bernice.

Zoe ran down the back steps and around the side of the house, jumping the corner of the Victory garden. She noticed that the weeds were thick among the vegetables. I'll weed later, she thought and raced into the front yard with a clatter of cans. Her mother's face appeared at the living-room window. Zoe waved. "We're going to the armory!" she yelled.

"We?" said Joe Bunch. "Who asked you?"

"Who wants our cans?"

"O.K., but you have to help pull the wagon on hills."

"I'm coming too," said Rosie.

Zoe considered this. If she didn't take Rosie along, Rosie would run right into the house and tell their mother. Then neither of them would be able to go. "O.K.," Zoe said. "But you have to pull, too."

"I will. Wait, though. I've got to get something," said Rosie.

"It's awful being the oldest," Zoe said to Joe while they waited. "I always have to take Rosie along. I have no privacy." Zoe scowled at the house. "You know what she's doing right now? She's in there getting this tiny little falling-apart doll. She can't go anywhere without it. She gets nervous. And all the time we have to stand here and roast waiting for her."

"Oh, well," Joe said.

"Oh, well, yourself! You'd hate it if Rosie was your sister."

"Rosie's not so bad," said Joe.

"She's awful!" Zoe kicked the wagon.

"Hey! Watch the cans!" Joe said. "Anyway, you could be nicer to Rosie."

"I don't notice you being so pie-nice to your brothers."

"My brothers stink."

Rosie came out the front door patting the pocket of her shorts. It bulged with her doll. The doll was supposed to be a secret and for a minute Zoe felt sorry for having told Joe. Sometimes, for no good reason, usually when she saw Rosie from a distance, she felt like hugging her. The feeling always surprised her. It was like waking up in the morning and not remembering what day it was.

"O.K.," said Rosie, "I'm ready."

"Give the wagon a shove to get it started," Joe said. "Then we can coast it to the corner."

They trotted along in front of the wagon trying to keep it from rolling too fast. The tin cans clattered and rattled going over bumps. Rosie puffed along behind. The street was hot and dusty and Zoe began wishing she were back on her front porch. The trouble about doing things with Joe was that they were usually uncomfortable. They were often exciting and always better than anything she could think of alone, but they weren't easy. The time they had climbed through the sewer pipe looking for old diamond rings that had washed down people's drains had been thrilling. But the sewer had smelled awful and she'd ruined her new school shoes. They'd never found any rings, either. Really they hadn't expected to find any. A lot of things they did Zoe knew were just pretend. It made them nicer. In a way it would have ruined the game if they'd really found a ring. She didn't know why that was true. It just was.

"Can we rest at the next corner?" she asked.

"Do you think our soldiers sit down in the middle of battle if they get tired?" Joe said. But at the next corner they did sit down under a hickory tree. Joe rearranged the cans and then flopped onto his stomach. "Boy, is this a wonderful summer!" he said.

"What?" Zoe was amazed.

"Wonderful," Joe said. "I've got all this work to do for the War and besides I'm planning to expand."

"Expand what?"

"My war work!"

"How?" Zoe asked.

"I haven't decided yet. I'm getting kind of tired of collecting cans and papers. I'm thinking of doing something really big. Trapping spies, for instance."

"Where are there any?" Zoe asked.

"Oh, all over. Anyone could be a spy. A spy's just an enemy agent. You could be one, except I know you're not."

"But I could help look for them."

"I don't know," said Joe. "I'd sort of planned to work alone."

"We could have a club," Zoe said. "We could call it the Looking-for-Spies Club."

"No," Joe said. "It'd turn out like all our other clubs. You'd want to have officers and bylaws and parliamentary procedure and we'd spend all summer just getting organized."

"You could be president if that's what's worrying you," Zoe said.

"Why do we have to have a club? Why can't we just look for enemy agents without all the fuss?"

"We can. We need some guidelines is all. Like, for instance, what's an enemy agent?"

"Oh, that's nothing. I can figure that out. What you do is watch for suspicious behavior. When you see somebody acting strange you trail him. You watch his movements. I'll figure out what to do after that. The main thing is to find the person."

Zoe smiled. She didn't really believe they'd find any

spies. Probably Joe didn't believe it either. The only person dumb enough to believe they would find spies was Rosie.

"What about Rosie?" Zoe looked at her sister sitting on the grass, peacefully searching for four-leaf clovers. She looked innocent enough, but she'd overheard everything for sure.

"I'm going to do it too," Rosie said.

"We'll have to let her," Zoe said crossly.

"That's all right," Joe said. "I'll figure out a job for Rosie."

"I'm small," said Rosie. "I can fit in places where nobody else can."

"It's true. She can," Zoe agreed. "She can fit in our clothes chute."

"She might come in handy," Joe said thoughtfully. "Plenty of times you need to get in small spaces for this work."

Rosie grinned. Her new front teeth gleamed. Zoe couldn't get used to seeing them. They were enormous and had jagged edges. Lately, when Rosie smiled, she reminded Zoe of a steam shovel.

Joe Bunch stood up. "We'd better get these cans delivered," he said. Rosie scrambled to her feet, then checked her pocket to be sure her doll was still there. Joe and Zoe got the wagon rolling again. "Keep your eyes open," Joe said. "You never know where you'll see a spy."

(2)

At the corner of Underwood Street and Happy Hollow Boulevard there was a vacant lot. Around the edges it was like any other vacant lot—full of candy-bar wrappers and black-eyed Susans—but in the middle there was a big patch of sumac. The sumac had thick brown stalks and ragged leaves that turned scarlet in the fall as though a flock of cardinals were roosting in the branches. Zoe didn't like the sumac much. The bushes were too tall. Once when she was younger she had tried to take a short cut through the patch. She'd gotten lost in the middle and for a while she'd thought maybe she was just going to die there. Of course, she'd found her way out finally, but she'd been all scratched and bloody.

Joe Bunch stopped at the edge of the lot and squinted his eyes. "Let's cut across," he said.

"We could," said Zoe, "but what'll happen is we'll get lost in the sumac."

"Oh, good grief!" Joe said. "How could we?"

"Listen, Joe, that sumac is way over our heads."

"Well, I'm going through it," Joe said.

"Well, I'm not." Once she'd said it Zoe wished she hadn't, because now she'd have to stick by it. In a way

23

she knew it was dumb to be scared of the sumac. She'd been much smaller when she got lost. Still, she hated it. The thing was, she was a coward.

"O.K., take the long way round. I'm going through the sumac," Joe said. He gave the wagon a yank and started clattering off across the vacant lot. Rosie stood watching a minute and then she set off after him.

"You'll get lost!" Zoe yelled, but neither of them paid any attention. Joe stalked along tugging the wagon and Rosie marched right after him, swatting black-eyed Susans. "You will!" Zoe yelled. "Just wait!"

She watched them disappear into the sumac, walking steadily. The last thing she saw were Rosie's red shorts. Neither of them even looked back. "Well!" Zoe said. She was mad.

Probably they wouldn't get lost. That was the worst part of it. They'd beat her to the armory and she'd have to hear about it the rest of the day. The only thing to do, she thought, is to beat them.

Zoe began running. It was five blocks to the armory but there were two places where you could cut through alleys. Zoe did that. She saw several good tin cans, but there was no time to pick them up. She dodged down the alleys, jumped over a cat, and arrived at the armory so hot and out-of-breath she was afraid she might faint. I wonder if eleven is too young to have a heart attack, she thought.

She had beaten them, though. They were not in the armory. They weren't even in sight. Zoe sat down on the armory steps to catch her breath. At first she felt good.

Then she started thinking. They could have urged her a little. They didn't care whether she came with them. It made her mad. She watched the people walking past and wondered if any of them really were enemy agents. It was hard to tell. If you watched long enough they all looked suspicious. It was like the time in the sewer. If you were thinking hard about diamonds, pretty soon every sparkle looked like one. She wondered if Joe might possibly know what he was talking about this time. She doubted it.

She stood up and peered down the street. They were nowhere in sight. Well, they *are* lost, she thought. She had a deep, crabby feeling of satisfaction. Maybe she wasn't brave, but at least she had common sense. She'd just walk up to the vacant lot and when Joe and Rosie finally found their way out of the sumac, all scratched and cut-up, she'd be standing there smiling. She knew the kind of smile she wanted. She'd seen it in the movies. You barely turned up the corners of your mouth. A person might have to look twice to know you were smiling. A year ago she'd have said, "See? I told you," but this year she was subtle. She practiced the smile several times before she set off.

The walk back seemed short. Zoe entertained herself by making up stories. She made up a long one about saving Rosie and Joe. By the time she reached the vacant lot, her deed was in headlines in the evening paper:

BRAVE GIRL SAVES CHILDREN IN DISTRESS

She was just receiving a bronze medal from the governor

when she noticed the wagon glittering at the edge of the sumac patch.

Zoe was startled. Where had they gone? It wasn't like Joe Bunch to leave his cans unprotected. Supposing Rosie was hurt! Zoe had a sudden awful feeling in her stomach. Rosie was so little! Zoe was scared. She ran toward the wagon.

When she reached it, there was still nobody in sight, but at least there wasn't any blood around. "Rosie! Joe!" Zoe called. "Joe! Rosie!" Nothing. She wondered whether she ought to look for them in the sumac. She was afraid to go into it alone. If she didn't see them soon she'd *have* to look in the sumac. First, she thought, I'll look around the edges.

She crept along the edge of the patch, ducking under the low branches. Twigs caught in her hair and gnats flew in her eyes. She walked face-first into a spider web. "Agh!" she said. She hated spiders. Then, while she was pulling the sticky web from her cheeks, up walked Fang. "Fang!" Zoe cried, "Where are they?"

Fang wasn't a very smart dog. He stood wiggling and panting, looking at Zoe with his good eye. "Show me where Joe is!" Zoe said. She knew better. Fang couldn't find a stick if you threw it a foot away. Still, if Fang was around, Joe was around.

Zoe shaded her eyes and looked about her. Way off in the corner of the lot under a lilac bush she saw a flash of red. Rosie's shorts! "Hey, Joe! Rosie!" she yelled, "Hey! What are you doing?" She was so relieved to see them she forgot to be angry. "Hey!" she called again.

From under the lilac bush Joe's head appeared. He scrambled out, waving his arms. "Joe!" she screamed. "What are you doing?" He waved his arms harder and shook his head. Zoe thought he looked like a windmill.

It's the silliest thing I've ever seen, Zoe thought. He's acting crazy.

Both Joe and Rosie were lying flat on their stomachs in the weeds by the time Zoe got close to them. "What are you two doing?" she asked, tripping over Fang as she reached them and stumbling into the lilac bush.

Joe's face was red and furious. "We happen to be trailing an enemy agent. Do you think you could shut up?" he whispered fiercely.

"How was I supposed to know that?" Zoe said.

"Be quiet!" Joe hissed. "Come on, Rosie." Rosie squirmed out from under the bush, looking important. Joe gave her a shove and the two of them began inching along through the weeds on their stomachs. Zoe dropped down and followed them. She couldn't see where they were going but she hoped it wasn't far. There were burrs on the ground, also bugs and probably snakes. Joe hitched along slowly, now and then sticking his head above the weeds to look around. Finally he stopped and sat up. "We lost him," he said. "All that yelling I guess."

"Well, how did I know not to yell?" Zoe said.

"O.K. But listen, Zoe, we found a real enemy agent, I'm positive of it."

"Yup," said Rosie.

Joe's eyes glittered. "Rosie and I were coming out of the sumac. We saw this man down by the apple tree.

Right away I knew he was suspicious. I guess I have a kind of instinct for it. So I said, 'Rosie, that's an enemy agent.' Right, Rosie?"

Rosie shrugged. "You said, 'Look at that man,' is what you said."

"Well, anyway. So we dropped to the ground and watched. He walked right up to the tree and stuck a note in that hole in the trunk."

"Then what?" Zoe asked. She tried to sound unimpressed.

"Well, then nothing," Joe said impatiently. "He walked away. Rosie and I started to follow him. That's when you came along yelling."

"How do you know he was an enemy agent? Just because he put a paper in a tree doesn't mean he's a spy."

"What else could he be? Think about it. Who else would be putting notes in a dead tree in a vacant lot?"

"Maybe," Zoe said.

"Maybe nothing. It's practically definite. But here's the best part, Zoe. Do you know who he was?" Joe's eyes were big as quarters. "That man was Miss Lavatier's boyfriend!"

"The gangster?" Zoe was getting excited.

"Yes. But I think I was wrong about that. I think he's been an enemy agent all along."

Zoe snorted. That was how Joe started projects. He forced things to fit the way he wanted them to. It made Zoe mad. "You don't even know he's her boyfriend," she said. "I don't think people that old *have* boyfriends. I mean Miss Lavatier's almost as old as our mothers."

"Well, for your information, he *is* her boyfriend. I saw him kiss her."

"On the lips?"

"Sure, on the lips. They were sitting right out on her porch swing."

"Still, that doesn't mean he's a gangster or a spy."

"Boy, if I was as unpatriotic as you are I'd worry,"

Joe said. "He's got to be an enemy agent. It's just obvious to everyone but you."

Zoe was beginning to believe it even though she knew it was silly. "We'd better call the police then," she said.

"Are you crazy?" Joe asked indignantly. "We have to have evidence. We can't accuse someone of being a spy without more evidence than we have."

"Let's get the note. That would be evidence."

Joe looked nervous. "I kind of want to think things over first," he said. "I'll come back and get it later. First we have to get organized, figure out a plan and all. Next we'll get the evidence and then we'll call the police. Maybe we'll call the FBI."

People probably get medals for catching spies, Zoe thought. She wondered whether there would be three medals or only one large one. She supposed there would be a ceremony with speeches and flowers. She wondered whether her blue organdy dress still fit. "The FBI?" she said.

"Why not? Catching an enemy agent isn't exactly nothing you know."

Zoe nodded slowly. That was true. "You'll get the note?" she asked.

"Leave that to me," Joe said. "The main thing now is to keep it all secret. If word gets out we're after that man, of course he'll just disappear."

"Got that, Rosie?" said Zoe.

Rosie looked solemn. She nodded. "I'm trustable," she said.

"All right," said Joe, "it's settled then. Remember," he added darkly, "keep mum. Anyone might be an enemy." Rosie nodded again. Zoe shivered in spite of herself.

(3)

Rosie and Zoe were in the bathtub. Their mother took one look when they got home and sent them straight upstairs. "You two look as though you crawled to the armory," she said.

Downstairs Bernice was singing "Praise the Lord and Pass the Ammunition" while she cooked. Bernice had a boyfriend in the Army so she was almost as patriotic as Joe Bunch. She wrote her boyfriend every day on little pieces of thin blue paper called V-mail. The paper was so thin that if Zoe held it up to the light on the way to the mailbox she could read what Bernice had written. Mostly what Bernice wrote was boring.

Rosie was scrubbing her knee with a nail brush. Zoe sat at the other end of the tub with the water faucet digging into her spine. They were getting too big to fit into the tub together. Still, it was more fun than being alone. Alone in the tub there was nothing to do but wash. Together they could play games. One was called Beautiful Mermaid. Rosie would lie in the water with her hair floating and pretend to be the drowning victim of a shipwreck. Zoe was the beautiful mermaid who saved her. Lately Rosie had wanted to be the mermaid and it was ruining the game.

Zoe looked at Rosie, soapy and glistening. "Want to play Beautiful Mermaid?" she said.

"Nope." Rosie began scrubbing the other knee.

"Sponge races?"

"No."

"What's the matter? You always want to."

"I'm thinking," Rosie said. "I'm wondering if I could fit in that hole in the apple tree."

"Well, of course you couldn't. You must be crazy. Fang wouldn't fit in that hole."

"I'm a terrible age," Rosie said. "You're lucky you don't have to be eight again. Nobody thinks I know anything, but I'm too big to fit in holes."

"You can still get in the clothes chute," Zoe said. "Listen, Rosie, was it really that man we always see at Miss Lavatier's?"

"Oh, yes, I recognized him right away," Rosie said. She was soaping her neck, doing a thorough job. "He was leaning on the apple tree and he was wearing that same white hat."

"And then he put a note in the tree?"

"I didn't see him do that. Joe says he did, though. I thought he was just leaning on the tree. Then he walked away."

"You mean he *didn't* put in a note?" Zoe was getting suspicious again.

"I don't know. Maybe I didn't see. I had to lean over and itch once."

34

Zoe was thoughtful. She pulled out the bathtub stopper slowly.

"I'm not rinsed!" Rosie said.

Zoe stood up and reached for her towel. "I wonder whether Joe made it up," she said. "What we should have done is to look for the note right then."

From downstairs came the smell of chicken frying and the sound of Bernice's voice. "Don't sit under the apple tree/with anyone else but me," she sang. Bernice sang one of two songs. This was the other one. The bath water disappeared with a final slurp. "I wasn't through," Rosie said crossly, but she got out and wrapped herself in a towel.

"Rosie, do you think Joe made it up about the note?" Zoe asked.

"I don't know. Why do you care?"

"Because if that man *didn't* put a note in the tree, he isn't suspicious. What's so suspicious about leaning on a tree?"

"Well, he could still be a gangster," Rosie said. She had got out the talcum powder and was patting it on her stomach. The room was slowly clouding with powder. Zoe sneezed.

"Rosie, you have no logic," she said. She gathered her clothes and went out, banging the bathroom door.

"Almost time for dinner," her mother called. "Daddy will be home soon."

Zoe went into her room. She put on a clean pair of shorts and a striped shirt. She stood sideways and looked at herself in the mirror. Her stomach stuck out. She pulled it in and gave herself a beautiful movie-star smile. "The Lovely Star of the Silver Screen at Play," she murmured. Zoe planned to be a famous journalist when she grew up and she spent a lot of time practicing headlines.

From Rosie's room came sounds of the radio warming up. It never came on directly, but rattled and hissed for several minutes, as though being turned on insulted it.

Rosie was going to listen to "Jack Armstrong, All-American Boy," her favorite program. She thought Jack Armstrong was a real person, which, of course, he wasn't. "There is no Jack Armstrong," Zoe had told her a million times. "He's just made-up."

"I don't care. I believe in him," Rosie always said. And she did. She sat in front of the radio and looked at it while she listened as if she expected to see Jack Armstrong come walking out. Zoe stood in the doorway watching her sister. Rosie was listening, sitting naked, covered with powder.

"You'd better get dressed," Zoe said. "Dinner's almost ready."

"Shhhh," Rosie whispered, staring at the radio.

"He isn't real!" Zoe shouted. She turned and walked out. Sometimes Rosie drove her crazy. It was no use telling her about Jack Armstrong or anything else. She thought what she thought. Period.

Zoe walked downstairs slowly, dragging her hand along the banister spokes. On the front-hall table was a crystal bowl of red and yellow roses. Next to it was the evening paper still folded in thirds. Zoe thought she might as well read the comics while she waited for dinner. She wanted to see what had happened to Smilin' Jack. She unfolded the paper carefully because her father hated to come home and find it mixed up. She was about to turn to the comic page when she noticed the headline:

FBI TRACES ENEMY AGENT TO
MIDWESTERN CITY

Underneath was a smaller headline: *Investigate Possibility of Axis Spy Ring.* Zoe dropped to her knees on the rug and smoothed out the front page. She read the article carefully. The government thought it had found a lot of spies, the paper said, but it wasn't saying where they were. Undisclosed Midwestern city. Well, Zoe thought, *this* is a Midwestern city. I wonder whether Joe Bunch has read the paper.

She stood up and put the paper back on the table. "Mother!" she shouted. "Mama! What's an axis?"

"Hmmm?" Her mother was in the living room.

"An axis. What is it?" Zoe asked, leaning against the living-room door.

"Well, it's a stem something revolves on. I mean, the earth has one. A kind of stalk, I think. Ask Daddy."

That doesn't make any sense—a stalk. What does the FBI want with a stalk? Zoe thought crossly. Grownups talked in code. She wondered whether it was something you caught on to as you grew taller.

Bernice came to the hall door to call them for dinner.

At the same minute their father's old black Packard pulled into the driveway. Rosie came dancing down the stairs as light as a ballerina. Their father hurried across the front lawn and up the porch steps. Good, thought Zoe, he didn't notice the Victory garden. He kissed everybody and dropped a pile of X-ray films on the hall table. "It's going to be ninety-five tomorrow," he said.

At dinner Zoe waited until the butter had melted into a yellow pool in her mashed potatoes. Then cautiously she made a trench in the potatoes so that the butter could run onto her ear of corn. She had to be careful. She was not supposed to play with her food. They ought to be glad I'm saving butter, she thought. She half listened to her parents talking until they were quiet for a minute. Then she said, "Daddy, what's an axis?"

"I told her to ask you," her mother said. "A kind of stem, I said."

"Right. The earth turns on an axis," her father said.

"Well, then what's an axis spy ring?" Zoe asked.

"Oh, that kind!" her mother said.

"The Axis is a name for the enemy countries," said her father. "Germany, Japan, and Italy are called the Axis powers. An Axis spy ring would be a group of spies for those countries."

"You mean there might be German or Japanese spies in this country? In this town even?" Zoe asked.

"There could be. Certainly there are spies in this country anyway."

Zoe took a bite of mashed potato. She was thinking hard. She knew she had to be careful asking questions if she weren't to give everything away. "Then why don't they get caught?" she said.

"Some do. But it's hard to tell who's a spy. That's the point. A spy could be anybody."

"Except Japanese spies would look Japanese. Right?"

"No. There are Americans who sympathize with Japan or Germany. They live in this country and some of them are spies."

"You mean it could be someone we know? A neighbor even?" Zoe felt excited but she tried not to sound that way.

"I suppose it could be."

Rosie's eyes had been getting wider. Suddenly she put down her ear of corn. "We weren't supposed to talk about it!" she said.

"I read about spies in the paper, for your information," said Zoe.

"Well, Joe Bunch said it was a secret!"

"Said what was, dear?" their mother asked.

Zoe kicked Rosie under the table.

"She kicked me!" Rosie cried. "She kicked me hard!"

"I did not. I was just swinging my leg," Zoe said.

"She meant to!" said Rosie. "She wanted me not to tell!"

"Not to tell what, for heaven's sake?" their mother asked.

Zoe had to kick Rosie again.

"She did it again! Right now! She just did it!" Rosie cried.

"Quiet!" Their father pounded his fist on his place mat. "You may both leave the table unless this stops!" Rosie picked up her corn and began to eat, watching Zoe with one eye over the cob.

"Some children aren't having any dinner at all tonight," their mother said.

"The War children," said Rosie. "They're starving."

"You girls ought to be thankful for food to eat," their father said, "and eat it without fighting."

"I am," Rosie said sweetly. "I am *so* thankful." Zoe would have liked to punch her. She could not understand why her parents didn't know Rosie was a phony.

"Rosie's just saying that. She doesn't really care," Zoe said.

"I do too!" cried Rosie.

"Phony!" Zoe yelled.

"That will be enough." Their father stood up. "You may take your plate to the kitchen."

"What about Rosie!" Zoe yelled.

"*I* will worry about Rosie."

There was no use arguing. Zoe picked up her plate and her glass of milk and went through the swinging door into the kitchen.

"Get sent away from the table again?" Bernice asked.

"Yes."

"Here. Sit down with me and finish your supper."

"I'm not hungry."

40

"Look at all that good food going to waste!" Bernice shook her head. "It's a crime. Think of the little children starving overseas!"

Zoe slammed her plate on the kitchen table. "Wrap it up and send it to them, Bernice!" she yelled. She ran out the back door, slamming that, too. What made her really mad was that she was still hungry. She could imagine Rosie in the dining room about to eat blueberry pie, probably with ice cream. It was unfair. After all, she'd only been trying to get information. If Rosie wasn't so stupid she'd have seen that. Zoe could hardly wait until some official was pinning on her medal. "What about my little sister?" she'd ask. "Doesn't she get one?"

"I'm terribly sorry," the official would say. "We can't give these medals to just anyone."

It'd serve her right, Zoe thought. She walked over to the Victory garden and ate a radish. It burned her tongue, but she felt better. She wanted to think things over.

If both her father and the newspaper said there could be spies anywhere, maybe Joe Bunch wasn't so crazy. Maybe the man he'd seen really was a spy. He certainly sounded suspicious all right. Funny that he was Miss Lavatier's boyfriend.

Zoe wandered around the side of the house. She began to feel much better. It was her favorite time of day. The street was quiet except for the swishing of sprinklers. In half an hour, when people had finished their suppers, the street would be busy again. Mrs. Nutt would come out on her porch and rock until dark. Mr. Powell, down the street, would dig crab grass with his pocketknife. One by one children would appear until there were enough of them for a game of kick-the-can. The whole block would be busy again until the streetlights came on. But right now for a few minutes Zoe had the street to herself.

Almost.

Down the block she saw Miss Lavatier come out her front door. She sat down on her porch swing with the newspaper. Zoe wondered whether Miss Lavatier knew her boyfriend was an enemy agent. If Joe Bunch was an enemy agent, wouldn't I know it? she thought. Of course I would. Miss Lavatier must know, too, unless she's awfully dumb. Zoe kicked a pebble along the sidewalk. If I had a conversation with Miss Lavatier, maybe I could find out something about her boyfriend, she thought. Wouldn't Joe Bunch be surprised if I did?

There would never be a better time—just Miss Lavatier and herself alone on the whole street. She gave the pebble another kick and sent it skittering into the grass. She wondered whether she really should do it. Well, why not? she thought. She walked casually toward Miss Lavatier's.

(4)

Zoe was so close to Miss Lavatier's house that she could hear the newspaper rattle when Miss Lavatier turned a page. Suddenly she wondered how she would start the conversation. She paused on the sidewalk to think it over.

Starting a conversation with Miss Lavatier wasn't going to be easy. Most of what Zoe knew about her she couldn't bring up. She knew Miss Lavatier's boyfriend was an enemy agent, that Joe Bunch thought Miss Lavatier lived in an empty house, and that Zoe's mother had called her pink awnings an eyesore. None of that would do. Probably she could mention the weather, but she didn't think that would lead to much.

Zoe was almost ready to forget the idea and go back home when she remembered something. Miss Lavatier taught tap dancing. It was the kind of thing that was easy to forget. Miss Lavatier didn't look like a tap-dancing teacher, but Zoe knew some girls who took lessons from her.

Zoe smiled to herself. That was it. She could ask about tap-dancing classes. She could pretend she was interested

in taking lessons. She stuffed her hands into the pockets of her shorts and strolled toward the house. She whistled softly, feeling clever.

"Hi, Miss Lavatier," she called when she was even with the porch. "Nice evening, isn't it?"

Miss Lavatier put down the newspaper and peered over the porch railing. "Yes. It's very nice," she said and picked up the paper again.

"It probably feels good to sit down after tap dancing all day," Zoe called.

"Yes, it does." Miss Lavatier smiled a little and kept reading. The conversation wasn't moving along quite the way Zoe had planned.

"Kind of hot weather for tap dancing," Zoe said, moving nearer the porch.

"Yes." Miss Lavatier did not smile. Zoe began to wish she hadn't thought of this plan, but by now she had got as far as the porch steps.

"Did you want something, dear?" Miss Lavatier asked. She peered over her reading glasses at Zoe. Zoe thought she looked kind of like a rabbit.

"Oh, well—I just thought we could talk, converse, you know. About tap dancing, I mean."

"Are you interested in tap dancing?" Miss Lavatier asked.

"Yes, I am," said Zoe. "I have always been interested in tap dancing. It's kind of a secret ambition of mine."

"How interesting," Miss Lavatier said, putting the paper down. "I give lessons, as you know."

45

"I knew that," Zoe said. "I've seen you out on the porch lots of times. I thought you looked like a good tap dancer."

"Thank you."

"I've seen you on your porch with people. I mean sometimes I see one of your friends out on the porch, too."

"Really?" said Miss Lavatier.

Oh, boy, Zoe thought, this was a terrible idea. She couldn't see any way to get from tap dancing to Miss Lavatier's boyfriend. She couldn't see any way to leave and go home either. What she had to do was change the subject.

"How do you think the War's going, Miss Lavatier?" she said.

Miss Lavatier looked at her oddly. "How do *I* think the War's going? Why do you ask?" she said.

"Oh, no reason," Zoe said. "I just thought I'd ask. I saw you were reading the paper. I suppose you've read about the Axis spy ring in the undisclosed Midwestern city."

"Yes," Miss Lavatier said. Zoe thought she looked suspicious.

"Well, I just thought I'd ask what you thought about it," Zoe said.

"I see," said Miss Lavatier. "That seems a very grown-up subject for someone your age."

"The War's kind of one of my hobbies," said Zoe. "I like to talk about it."

Miss Lavatier smiled her little rabbit smile and picked

up the paper again. "We'll have to talk sometime," she said.

"That would be fine!" said Zoe. "I'm free most days this summer, so any time suits me. I can stop by tomorrow."

"Well, maybe not tomorrow, but we'll work out something."

When Miss Lavatier smiled, Zoe couldn't help thinking about how Joe had seen that man kissing her on the lips. It was hard to imagine. She wondered if Miss Lavatier shut her eyes like in the movies. "I know you're busy most evenings," she said, "with friends and all."

"I'm often here in the afternoons," Miss Lavatier answered. Zoe could see that she was dying to read the paper. Probably that was enough information for the first visit anyway.

"Well, be seeing you, Miss Lavatier," Zoe said. She began backing off the porch steps.

"Yes. By the way, I have a class for beginners Saturday mornings. You might mention it to your mother."

"O.K., I will, Miss Lavatier," Zoe said. She had no intention of doing it. The worst thing she could think of was tap dancing all Saturday morning. Still, she was pleased with the conversation. She hadn't found out much about Miss Lavatier's boyfriend, but she had mentioned the War and the spy ring. Miss Lavatier had definitely acted peculiar when she did that. Zoe glanced back over her shoulder at the porch swing. Maybe Miss Lavatier herself was a spy. You never could tell.

When Zoe got home Joe Bunch was sitting on the

grass waiting for her. Fang was sprawled on the sidewalk. "What were you doing down at Miss Lavatier's?" Joe asked suspiciously.

"War work," said Zoe.

"Like what?" Joe said. "You'd better not have let on about anything."

"Oh, honestly!" Sometimes Joe made her mad. "You can trust me, I think," she said.

"So what did she say?" Joe took a small notebook and a pencil stub from his pocket.

"What's that for?" Zoe asked.

"To keep a record. It's business-like. We have to keep a complete record of the evidence," Joe said. "See, I've written down all the evidence so far."

Zoe looked at the notebook. On the first page Joe had written WAR WORK in large block letters in red and blue crayon. On the next page he had written the date and under it all about seeing Miss Lavatier's boyfriend in the vacant lot.

"What about the note? There's nothing in here about going back to get the note," Zoe said.

"It wasn't there, that's why. I was just about to tell you."

Zoe looked at Joe suspiciously. "Rosie says she didn't see any note."

"Well, *I* saw it. I saw that guy put a note in the tree and when I went back to get it, it was gone. Somebody else picked it up, Zoe!"

"Like another enemy agent, you mean?"

"What else?"

Zoe was doubtful. "Maybe you're right," she said.

"Of course I'm right! We're really onto something big this time. But I gotta have the evidence you got from Miss Lavatier now before my father calls me."

"Do you want the whole conversation? I'm not sure I can remember everything."

"The important parts. We can leave out 'Hello' and 'Good-by' and that stuff," Joe said.

"All right, then. She said she'd seen the thing about enemy agents in the paper and, Joe, she had the strangest expression when she said it."

"Aha!" Joe Bunch bent over his notebook. Then he looked up. *He* had a strange expression. "What thing in the paper?" he said.

"Didn't you read it?"

Joe looked funny. "Haven't had time," he said. "Plan to do it later."

"I'll tell you about it." Zoe felt kind. Joe Bunch was a terrible reader. He was always being tutored. Sometimes she forgot that.

She told him as much as she could remember about what she'd read. Then she told him what her father had said. Joe Bunch looked happier and happier. "This just about proves it," he said. "I kind of had an instinct I was right." He began to write in his notebook again. "How do you spell Axis?" he asked. "Oh, never mind. We have to put all this in code tomorrow anyway."

"Code?"

"Sure. What if someone got hold of this notebook? Do you want the Enemy to know what we're doing? Do you want some assassin after us?"

Zoe hadn't thought of that. "Will this be pretty dangerous, do you think?" she asked.

"Can't help but be," Joe said. "That's part of war work. Want to quit?"

"No." Zoe shook her head. She didn't want to quit, but she knew this would be like all Joe's schemes—uncomfortable, hard, and scary. She sighed. "No," she said, "I want to do it."

"All right," Joe said. "Then here's what we have to do tomorrow: First, we set up headquarters in the vacant lot. We can hide in the sumac patch and keep watch from there."

"Oh, Joe, there'll be snakes there!" Zoe said.

"Do you think our soldiers complain about a few snakes? Anyway, they're garter snakes," Joe said. "Now, second, we have to make a code. We can do that at headquarters after we get set up. And, third, we have to find out all about Miss Lavatier's boyfriend. That's the most important part."

Zoe nodded. She was still thinking about snakes. She didn't care if they were only garter snakes. She hated them.

"That'll be your job," Joe said.

"What will?" Zoe hadn't been listening.

"To find out about Miss Lavatier's boyfriend!" Joe said impatiently.

"My job! How in the world will I do that?" Zoe felt

tricked. Joe was always getting her to do the worst part of his projects.

"You're the one who knows Miss Lavatier," Joe said, "You'll just have to get to know her better. You're good at things like that, Zoe."

The screen door opened and Rosie came out onto the porch. She had a big blueberry stain on her shirt. "We have to get ready for bed," she said.

"Joe!" It was Mr. Bunch yelling from way down on Victoria Street.

"Gotta go," Joe said. "It's settled about your job then. Right, Zoe?"

"I guess so."

All up and down the street mothers and fathers began coming out to call their children in. Suddenly the street-lights came on. Zoe thought they looked like balloons floating above the sidewalk. Moths were battering them-selves against the screen door, trying to reach the hall light. It was time to go in.

Zoe stood up slowly. She scratched a mosquito bite. Down in front of Miss Lavatier's house she saw a truck pull up to the curb. She stared at it, wondering who it could be. She watched a man get out and walk up to the house. It was too dark to see much except his shoes and his hat glowing white in the streetlight. That must be her boyfriend, Zoe thought.

"Zoe!"

"Coming." Zoe took a last look and moved toward the door.

"Hurry on upstairs," her mother said. "It's late."

Zoe got into bed quickly. She waited for her mother and father to come up to kiss her. After she could hear them back in the living room again she crept to her window and peered at Miss Lavatier's porch. All she could see was the porch light. How would she find out anything about that man? Darn Joe Bunch! She didn't *want* to get to know Miss Lavatier. She watched for a while but nothing happened. Finally she tiptoed back to bed. She yawned. She hated to admit it, but in some ways trapping spies was making the summer more interesting.

(5)

The smell of bacon. The sound of a lawn mower.

Zoe opened her eyes. She sat on the edge of the bed and scratched her stomach where her pajamas gapped. She wondered who was cutting grass. She remembered Arnold who had cut their grass until he was drafted. She tried to imagine Arnold in an Army uniform but it was impossible. He wasn't the type.

She wandered into the hall. Rosie was up. Her flowered pajamas were on the floor in her room. Zoe slid down the banister, catching herself before she banged the newel post. She had always wished she had the nerve to slide down facing forward. Joe Bunch had slid down his banister forward once, flown right off the end, and hit the front door. He'd had a black tooth ever since. It wasn't worth it probably.

Everyone was in the breakfast room. Zoe stopped in the doorway and yawned. Her mother looked up. "We didn't know you were interested in tap dancing, dear," she said. Zoe halted in mid-yawn.

"What?" she said.

"Miss Lavatier phoned this morning. Apparently you talked to her about lessons?"

Zoe's mother was sitting at the breakfast table in her Red Cross uniform, counting ration stamps. "Well, what about it?" she said.

"I don't know."

"Miss Lavatier said tap dancing was your secret ambition. You should have told us that. Of course you must have lessons. Daddy and I had no idea you were interested."

Bernice was clearing the table. "Regular Ginger Rogers in the house and we never knew it," she said.

Rosie poked her head out from under the table where she was playing jacks. "I got past foursies," she said.

"What are you doing under there?" Zoe asked.

"Practicing playing jacks in an air raid."

Zoe got down on her knees. She thought she might feel better under the table herself. She crawled in beside Rosie next to her mother's foot.

"So shall I tell Miss Lavatier you'll be there Saturday?"

Zoe looked at the foot. She scratched her stomach. She knew Joe Bunch would want her to do it. It was a perfect opportunity to get to know Miss Lavatier. Still, she didn't think she could stand the lessons. "I don't know," she said, "maybe with the War and all I shouldn't."

"Listen, Zoe." It was Bernice's voice. "Maybe you'll tap so good they'll let you give a show down at the USO."

"Oh, boy, wouldn't *that* be wonderful," Zoe said. Bernice was such an idiot sometimes.

Her mother's face appeared upside down below the

hem of the tablecloth. "Yes or no?" she said. "I'm in a hurry. Don't worry about the War. That doesn't matter in this case."

"Do it, Zoe," Rosie said. "Maybe you could have a costume with diamonds on it."

"Well," Zoe said. She felt trapped. She had to have time to think. "Well, maybe," she said.

"Good. Then it's settled. I'll call Miss Lavatier after Red Cross." Her mother stood up and put on her Red Cross hat.

"I didn't say yes." Zoe crawled out. "Maybe I don't want to."

"Ummm." Mentally her mother was already out of the house. Then Mrs. Chase was honking in the driveway. "We'll see," her mother said and kissed the air twice in their direction.

"Oh, Zoe, are you ever lucky!" Rosie said. "You can have those black shoes with bows and learn the splits and everything!"

Zoe groaned.

"Who wants to do the margarine?" Bernice called.

Usually Zoe wanted to. Since butter was rationed they used margarine. It came white in a plastic bag and looked like lard. There was a yellow bead of dye in the middle like a vitamin pill. When you squeezed the bead, yellow dye came out. Rosie and Zoe took turns kneading the bag until the dye was blended and the margarine turned yellow. Finally, it looked like butter. It took a long time but it was fun.

"Let Rosie do it," Zoe said. Her life was getting much

too complicated. She had to go to her room to think.

Zoe's room was a mess as usual. Her bed was not made. Her shorts, shirt, and underpants were on the floor where she'd dropped them. She had spilled fish food on the rug. Part of the Monopoly money, two library books, a wishbone, a screw driver, an empty bottle of Evening in Paris cologne, and a copy of *Photoplay* were on her dresser. Under her bed were a charm bracelet and part of a doughnut. She found these two things while she was looking for her shoes.

I ought to clean up this room, Zoe thought. She sat on her bed and stared at the wallpaper. There was a jagged brown spot in one corner near the ceiling where she had thrown a bottle of iodine. She'd been aiming for Rosie.

The trouble is I have no coordination, Zoe thought. I missed Rosie by five feet with that iodine. It was the same with baseball. Tap dancing was out of the question. Zoe knew something about those lessons. Her friend Cozette Tweedy had shown her some of the steps they learned. All that tapping around was fine if you were coordinated like Cozette. I could sprain my ankle, Zoe thought.

She sighed. The trouble was, she knew it was her duty to take those lessons. Soldiers had to do terrible things for their country. I ought to be able to take a few dancing lessons, Zoe thought. I must be that patriotic. She knew this was the kind of thing Joe Bunch would say. Just then she heard the front door bang and

Joe's voice in the hall. In a way she wished she didn't even know him.

She found some shorts and a shirt. Checks and stripes. Her mother would have a fit. Oh, well. She dressed quickly and ran downstairs.

Joe and Rosie were in the kitchen finishing the margarine. Rosie had poked a hole in the plastic bag with her fingernail so that quite a bit of margarine had leaked out. Some of it was on Rosie.

"Ready?" said Joe. "We're already behind schedule."

"She has to eat first," Bernice said. "She has to have breakfast."

"Make me some toast, Bernice, and I can take it along," Zoe said.

"Nope. Bacon and eggs."

"I'll throw up. I'll definitely throw up, Bernice."

"At least cereal," Bernice said, setting a bowl before her. "We have to eat up this code-ring stuff." Zoe had been eating the same cereal all summer. She needed four box tops to order a secret code ring. She was on the third box.

Joe Bunch waited until Bernice left the room. Then he said, "Can't you eat any faster? I planned to have the headquarters set up by this time."

"I'm taking some peaches just in case," Rosie said.

"Someone has to be at headquarters from right after breakfast until dinnertime," said Joe. "I borrowed my father's binoculars."

"He let you have them?" Zoe was so surprised she stopped eating.

"When he finds out what a great service we did our country with his binoculars, he'll be glad I used them. I'm going to surprise him after we catch the agent. Also I brought a butcher knife for protection."

"Blood." Rosie murmured.

"I'm not stabbing anyone with a butcher knife!" Zoe said.

"I guess if some enemy agent sneaks up from behind and starts torturing you, you'll be glad to use it."

Zoe snorted. Sometimes Joe went too far.

He had loaded his wagon with furnishings for their headquarters. Besides the binoculars and the butcher knife he had brought two tablets of lined paper and three pencils, a folding chair, a pink blanket, a citronella candle, and a box of matches. There were also a stack of Captain Marvel comic books and half a box of saltines in the wagon.

"And my peaches, don't forget," Rosie said, "and my jacks."

When they were a block away from the vacant lot, Joe sent Rosie ahead to scout. "Be sure nobody's around," he said. "We don't want to be seen."

"That's called reconnoitering," he said to Zoe as they watched Rosie grow smaller and finally disappear around the corner, checking her pocket.

"How come you picked Rosie?"

"She's too little to pull the wagon, and, anyway, she has to have a job."

They were sitting on the wagon, trying to hide the

contents as best they could. Fang lay on the sidewalk, panting. The air buzzed. Zoe fanned herself with a comic book. "I wonder what's taking her so long," she said.

Joe grunted. He was working on the code in his Spiral notebook. "A is a circle, B is a cross, C is a dot, and D is a swastika," he said. "What about E?"

"You can't have a swastika," Zoe said. "That's an enemy sign. What if someone finds the notebook?"

"Well good grief, Zoe, that's the point. It's to confuse people. I mean, suppose someone tortures me and I have to give up the notebook. They'll see the swastika and think maybe I'm a German counterspy or something. I'm going to put in some Japanese stuff, too."

Rosie came running around the corner, grinning. "It's O.K.!" she called.

"Boy! One thing we have to do is teach her to be quiet," Joe said.

Rosie came panting up to them. "Does Mrs. Nutt count?" she asked. "She's the only person I saw."

"She's pretty nearsighted," said Zoe.

"O.K. We have to take some risks," Joe said. They put Fang on top of the load in the wagon and tried to make him lie down. Usually Fang liked lying down better than any other position, but this time he insisted on standing. He wavered on top of the load all the way down the street, around the corner, and up to the edge of the vacant lot. Mrs. Nutt was gone.

"All right. You two stand guard and I'll take the

wagon," Joe said. "If anyone comes along, whistle three times and I'll hide. I'll drop down in the grass. Then whistle twice when they're gone so I'll know."

"I can't whistle since I got my new teeth," Rosie said.

"You couldn't whistle before either," Zoe said.

"Sing then—good and loud. Or hum," said Joe.

Zoe took a position at the corner of the lot where she could see all the way down Happy Hollow Boulevard and part way up Underwood. Rosie stood at the other corner in the alley. Joe took out the binoculars and scanned the lot slowly. Then he headed for the sumac patch.

Zoe looked up Underwood and down Happy Hollow. There wasn't a soul on either street for as far as she could see. Joe was halfway to the sumac patch. Something must have fallen from the wagon. He had stopped to pick it up. Suddenly she heard Rosie's voice loud, almost screaming.

"Silent night! Holy night!" Rosie was singing. Joe fell to his knees and vanished in the high grass. "All is calm and all is—hello, Mr. Innes."

Zoe took a deep breath. It was just Mr. Innes, the postman. Mr. Innes was about eighty-five. She had known him all her life. Even so her legs shook. Mr. Innes came out of the alley with Rosie, who was still humming. "Pretty hot day for Christmas carols," Mr. Innes said. Rosie was looking around wildly. You never knew if you could trust Rosie. Sometimes when she was scared or confused she fell apart.

"Hi, Mr. Innes," Zoe said.

"You girls playing hide-and-seek?"

"Oh, we're just kind of hanging around."

"Pretty hot day for Christmas carols, I told your sister."

Zoe tried to laugh nonchalantly. "It's the only song she knows," she said.

"That's not true!" Rosie cried. "I know 'Sweet and Low' and 'It's a Long Way to Tipperary' all the way through by heart."

"You ought to be sitting in the shade," Mr. Innes said. "I wish I was." He hoisted his bag higher on his shoulder. "Heat wave," he added, "heat stroke."

Rosie and Zoe watched him cross the street, sorting a handful of letters. Finally Zoe decided it was safe. She whistled twice. Joe's head popped out of the grass. He looked around. Zoe waved. Joe scrambled up and hurried the wagon toward the sumac.

(6)

In five minutes they were all safe in the shade of the sumac branches. It wasn't as bad as Zoe had imagined. Rosie and Joe unpacked the wagon and Zoe arranged things. She spread the pink blanket on the ground like a carpet. At one corner she put the saltines, peaches, and butcher knife. Diagonally across she set up the folding chair and arranged the stack of comic books. "Just like a little house," she said, feeling pleased with her work. "Put the matches in the kitchen, Joe, until we need them."

"Kitchen!" Joe sounded disgusted. "We're not playing house. This is war work." Joe put the matches next to the saltines. "I'll finish the code and, Zoe, you take first watch." He handed her the binoculars. "There's a good spot over there. You can see the apple tree through that hole in the branches."

Zoe saw that there was a stump to sit on and a place where the sumac was thin enough to peek through. She took a peach and picked up the folding chair. "What are you doing that for?" Joe asked.

"I have to sit on something."

"Sit on the stump. Whoever heard of a spy on watch using a folding chair? Do you want to do this thing right or just any old which-way?"

"What about me?" said Rosie. "I want a job, too."

"This is your break, Rosie. You're supposed to take a nap. We're going to have two-hour watches. That's the way it's done. The people not watching rest." Joe sat down on the folding chair. Zoe slung the binoculars around her neck and walked off to her post.

By propping her elbows on her knees, her chin on her hands and resting the binoculars on her cheek bones and fingertips, Zoe could keep watch without working too hard. After ten minutes she began to wonder why she needed binoculars. She could see the apple tree perfectly without them. She glanced around at Joe. He was lying on the blanket writing in his notebook and paying no attention to her. Carefully she laid the binoculars on the ground at her feet. A lot of Joe's ideas were silly. She took a bite of peach and squeezed it against the roof of her mouth, pressing out the juice. She propped her chin in her hands and stared at the apple tree. In the field beyond the sumac the heat hung in the air like shivering cellophane. She began to feel sleepy. She stared at the tree without really seeing it. Her chin slipped and her head jerked. She sat up straight and took another bite of peach. War work was boring.

She raised the binoculars to have another look at the tree close up. She noticed a man walking along the sidewalk. At first she didn't pay much attention to him.

Then all at once she realized he was wearing a white straw hat. She caught her breath and looked again. It was Miss Lavatier's boyfriend and he was walking straight toward the apple tree! Suddenly Zoe was scared. Seeing him was different from imagining him. Her hands began to shake so the binoculars rattled. "Joe!" she whispered. "Joe!"

Joe jumped up and came running toward her in a crouch. "He's there!" she whispered. "I really sort of thought you made it up!"

"Give me the binoculars," Joe said. He squinted at the tree. "That's him! That's the same man! That's Miss Lavatier's boyfriend!"

Together they crept closer to the edge of the sumac patch. They watched. The man rummaged in his pocket. He took out a piece of paper and leaned against the tree while he quickly scribbled something on it. Then he folded the paper and glanced around. Zoe could feel her heart beating in ten different places. Joe stared through the binoculars, biting his tongue. The man looked around again. Then he turned and dropped the paper into the hole in the apple tree. Zoe gasped. "Oh, Joe! He *is* an Enemy," she whispered.

"Sshh!" Joe punched her arm. The man had turned. He started to walk away quickly in the direction of the public library. "O.K.," said Joe, "get Rosie."

Zoe crept back to the blanket. She felt hollow in her stomach. She'd never really expected to see the Enemy again. She didn't want to see him. Not now. Maybe last night it had seemed exciting, but to see a real enemy spy at work—! Zoe swallowed hard.

Rosie really had fallen asleep. She lay curled up with her thumb in her mouth. Zoe shook her.

"Come on! Get up!" Zoe said.

"This is my rest period."

"Come on! We saw an Enemy."

"Where!" Rosie was wide awake and sitting up at once. "Where is he? Did you torture him yet?"

"No, dummy. We didn't exactly catch him yet."

Joe came over, swinging the binoculars. "He's out of sight. We have to get that note," he said.

"Remember, Joe, somebody's coming for it!" Zoe said.

"So we have to get it first," Joe said.

They crept out of the sumac into the sun, blinking. Zoe and Rosie followed Joe across the vacant lot, crouching low in the tall grass. This is awful, Zoe thought. This is the worst thing Joe's ever thought up.

They reached the apple tree and stood looking at the hole in the trunk. It was too high up. They couldn't reach it. "O.K.," Joe said. "We'll have to boost Rosie." Together Joe and Zoe gave Rosie a foot-up and then shoved her from behind until she could grab the edge of the hole. "Can you see it, Rosie?" Joe whispered.

"I need a flashlight," Rosie said. "It's deep in there and it's dark."

"Feel around."

Rosie squirmed farther up the tree trunk. She leaned

into the hole up to her waist. Her legs waved above them.

"See anything?" Joe said.

From inside the tree came noises of scratching and occasionally a grunt. Then out came one of Rosie's arms. She was holding the paper. "Drop it! Drop it!" Joe whispered. The paper came fluttering to the ground like a butterfly.

Joe and Zoe dropped to their knees in the tall grass.

Even Joe's hands were shaking as he unfolded the paper. "What is it? What does it say?"

"I don't know. It doesn't make sense," Joe said.

Just then there was an awful racket from inside the tree. "I'm stuck! Get me out of here!" Rosie cried. Her voice sounded as though it were coming from the end of a wet tunnel. "This isn't fair!" she cried. "There are bugs!" Her legs were waving and with her one free arm she was banging the tree trunk.

"O.K.," said Joe, "take it easy." He and Zoe each grabbed a leg and pulled.

"Ouch! Don't pull so hard! My arm's stuck!"

They wiggled and tugged at her until finally Rosie's head shot out of the hole like a bullet. She came plunging to the ground on top of them.

"Ouch!" Zoe yelled. "My gosh, Rosie, you didn't have to squash us."

Rosie was on her feet, adjusting her shorts. "You could say thank you," she said crossly.

"Thanks, Rosie," Joe was back on his knees examining the note.

"What is it? Let me see," Zoe said.

"Nobody cares if a person is in pain," Rosie grumbled. "A person could starve to death inside a tree."

"I think it's code," Joe said.

Zoe looked at the paper. Written on it were numbers: "3–8: 10–16" That was all. "But what does it *mean?*" she said.

"I don't know. It's code of some kind. I'm going to copy the numbers in my notebook."

"Let's just take the note and get out of here."

"No. We have to put it back. Someone's coming for it, don't forget."

"Oh!" Zoe felt herself begin to tremble. She'd forgotten that. "Well, hurry up! Maybe they're around right now, Joe."

Joe scribbled the numbers quickly on a fresh page. He refolded the note. "O.K., Rosie. We'll boost you back up and you can drop it in," he whispered.

"Nope."

"What do you mean?"

"I'm not going back in that tree. I think there was even a worm in there. I felt it."

"You don't have to crawl in again. Just drop the note."

Rosie scowled. "You'll forget me."

"Oh, good grief." Joe took the note and jumped. With a kind of hook shot he sent the paper flying into the hole. "All right, now run!" he said.

Zoe was already halfway back to the sumac patch. Rosie insisted on walking. They watched her approaching from inside the cover of the branches. "She thinks she's being dignified," Zoe said.

"She'll be all right. The thing about Rosie is she can't stay mad very long."

They flopped down on the pink blanket and waited for her. "When do we start torturing and all that?" Rosie asked, coming up to them. Zoe snorted.

"You've got it wrong, Rosie," Joe said. "We don't torture people. What we do is get information. Now, somebody's coming for that note, so we'll just lie here and watch. We need to know who it is."

They shared a peach while they waited. Mrs. Hall passed by on the sidewalk carrying a string bag with celery sticking out the top. Two third-graders went by on roller skates. Mrs. Innes's collie came sniffing around the edges of the sumac and Fang growled in his sleep. Zoe hoped nobody would come for the note. The more real the war work got, the more Zoe wished Joe had never thought of it. Maybe it would turn out that Miss Lavatier's boyfriend wasn't a spy after all. Maybe he just had an insane desire to put notes in apple trees. The more she thought about it, the likelier it seemed. She turned to Joe to tell him what she'd decided, but he wasn't listening. He grabbed her arm. He was staring at the apple tree, hardly breathing. "Look!" he whispered.

Zoe looked. Standing beside the tree, glancing first right, then left, was a fat man in a wrinkled gray suit. While they watched, he put his whole arm into the hole in the apple tree, fished around and pulled out the note. He put the paper into his pocket, looked around again, and hurried off down the sidewalk, almost running.

Zoe gulped. "Who *was* it?" she whispered.

"Never saw him before."

"I have," Rosie said. "That's Mr. Pear. I see him all the time when Daddy and I go down to the train station to get the New York paper."

"You made that up," Zoe said.

"I did not," said Rosie. "Go down there and see."

"We aren't allowed to go there alone."

"I'll go," Joe said. "Right after lunch. You two keep watch here. I don't mind going alone. I can stand danger."

Zoe sighed. Too much was happening. Things were getting too serious. "Maybe they aren't really spies," she said. "Maybe it's just a game or something."

Joe looked exasperated. "Why do you have to keep saying things like that?" he asked. "Sometimes having you around is like carrying a ten-ton rock on my head. If you're scared, say so. If you want out, just say so."

"I was being logical is all."

"You were being nutty. Here we are tracking some perfectly definite spies and you make up stupid theories like that. All you have to do is sit here in the sumac and watch that tree. I'm doing all the hard part."

Zoe stood up and tucked in her shirt. She felt embarrassed. Then she remembered the tap-dancing lessons and felt mad. "You're not the only one," she muttered, but she didn't explain what she meant.

"I'm going home," Rosie said. "I'm starving."

"Just be back here right after lunch," Joe said.

Zoe struggled through the sumac after Rosie. Joe followed behind. "Hey, I forgot," he said as they reached the edge of the patch, "that's really swell about the dancing lessons."

Zoe whirled around and stared at him. "How do you know about that?"

"I told him all about it while we were doing the margarine," Rosie said. "Only Joe doesn't think you'll get a costume with diamonds right away."

Zoe groaned. "Well, I may not do it," she said.

"What do you mean 'not do it'? It's a perfect chance to get information!" Joe said.

"I just may not, that's all."

Joe said nothing. He looked at her. Then he turned his back.

"I don't have to!" Zoe cried.

Joe snorted. "I guess there are some people around here who want the Japs to win the War. Right, Rosie?"

"Not me," Rosie said.

"Too bad one of your relatives doesn't feel that way." Joe gave Zoe a last look and walked off through the sumac. He didn't even say good-by.

Zoe sighed. She was done for. If she didn't take those lessons, Joe would be mad at her all summer. She knew she couldn't stand it.

(7)

Saturday morning was hot. Zoe could feel the heat from the sidewalk through the soles of her sneakers. She carried her new tap shoes in a paper bag. She was on her way to Miss Lavatier's studio.

It was all that stupid Rosie's fault. If Rosie hadn't mentioned tap dancing to Joe Bunch, Zoe wouldn't be on her way to Miss Lavatier's now. Well, she thought, it can't be any worse than sitting in the sumac patch.

She and Rosie had been sitting in the sumac patch all week. Thursday afternoon Rosie'd had to sit alone while Zoe had her braces tightened. That same afternoon Zoe got her tap shoes. They'd cost four clothing stamps, so that settled it about the lessons. My teeth ache, I'm taking dancing, and I have twenty-six mosquito bites on my right arm, Zoe thought. What a swell way to spend the summer.

The worst part was that all that sitting in the sumac had been for nothing. Not a thing had happened. Nobody had come near the apple tree. Part of the time Zoe had practiced writing newspaper articles. Part of the time she'd read Wonder Woman comics, but mostly it had been a waste of time.

Joe kept trying to decipher the note. Every day he had a new idea. As far as Zoe was concerned none of it made any sense. There wasn't much you could do with a few numbers.

Zoe was mad at Joe Bunch. She blamed him for everything but her teeth aching. He was the one who insisted they sit in that buggy sumac. He was the reason she was taking tap dancing.

"Is Joe Bunch getting bitten to pieces by bugs?" she said out loud. "Is he wasting a perfectly good Saturday morning? Oh, no, he's not! He's sitting down at the railroad station drinking Orange Crush." That was Joe's job, watching Mr. Pear sell tickets at the railroad station. Zoe suspected that he would never get any evidence that way. Personally she thought Joe just liked being comfortable.

LOCAL GIRL STABS FRIEND

Thinking up a headline always comforted her.

Zoe walked along with her eyes on the sidewalk. She stepped over cracks and avoided holes. She knew she was being superstitious, but she didn't like taking chances.

The quickest way from Zoe's house to Miss Lavatier's studio was across the square. The square was the middle of town. It was a grass patch with stores on all four sides. In the center was the statue of a Civil War soldier leaning on a gun. Long ago, when she was practically a baby, Zoe had thought that statue was the Holy Ghost. She was glad she'd never mentioned it to anyone. That was the kind of thing her mother would never forget. Suddenly at Thanksgiving dinner with about twenty-five relatives sitting around, her mother would say, "Zoe told me the funniest thing." There were enough of those things already.

Zoe cut across the square, swinging her paper bag. There were green wooden benches at intervals along the sidewalk. Between the benches were beds of dusty red cannas. Cannas were the ugliest flowers in the world. You couldn't kill them, Zoe's mother said, and that was why they were planted in public places.

Across the square Zoe could see Mr. Chase arranging boxes of strawberries on the stand outside his grocery store. There was a line of children waiting outside the Queenie Drugstore. Mr. Bunch must have gotten in some real bubble gum, Zoe thought.

Real bubble gum—the kind that made big strong bubbles that didn't stick to your face too badly when they popped—was rationed. There was plenty of phony bubble gum that tasted like cherry-flavored chalk, but the real thing was scarce. Zoe could hardly remember the time before the War when real bubble gum was plentiful.

She checked over the people in line. The only person she knew was Bill Grabb. She didn't know him well enough to ask him to buy her any and she hadn't time to stand in line. "You'd think Joe Bunch would have told me," she muttered crossly. After all, it was his father who was selling it.

Zoe turned the corner. Miss Lavatier's studio was

75

on the second floor of a building on Baldwin Street. There was a dentist's office on the first floor. Zoe could smell antiseptic as she climbed the stairs. She thought she could hear a drill. It made her teeth ache.

LILLIAN LAVATIER
Studio of the Dance
WALK IN

Well, this is it, Zoe thought. She walked in.

Inside were about ten girls in shorts and black-patent-leather tap shoes. Zoe recognized some of them. One was Opal Wheeler, the person Zoe hated most in the world. Boy, this is really superb, Zoe thought.

Miss Lavatier was taking attendance. She had on a sort of peach silk playsuit and, of course, tap shoes. "Oh, Zoe," she said, "I'm glad you're here. Did you bring shoes?"

Zoe nodded. She pulled her shoes out. "Fine. Get them on. We're ready to begin."

Opal Wheeler came sidling over to Zoe. "You going to take lessons?" she asked.

Zoe looked up. "No," she said, "I'm going to play basketball."

"Ha-ha."

"Well, what do you think I'm going to do, Opal?"

"I just asked. My gosh, a person has a right to ask, don't they? It's a free country."

Zoe stuffed her foot into her tap shoe. I better get a lot of information, she thought, because if I don't I'm going to walk right out of here.

"I didn't know you were in our class," Opal said.

"I am."

"Well, I can see that, I hope. Did your mother make you, or what?"

Zoe didn't answer.

"My mother wants me to get graceful," Opal said. "That's why I take dancing—to get graceful. Also to get poise."

"My mother wants me to get in the movies," Zoe said sarcastically.

"Oh, ha! You think you're so funny." Opal did some kind of tap step that looked complicated to Zoe. Then she walked away.

"All right girls, line up." Miss Lavatier led them into a square room with a shiny wood floor. There were large mirrors on all four walls. Miss Lavatier put a record on the phonograph and stood holding the needle poised. We'll do brush–brushes first," she said. "Zoe, you haven't done these, so watch a minute. It's very simple. You'll catch on."

Miss Lavatier started the music. Zoe watched. "All right, girls. Brush–brush and brush–brush and—" It looked pretty easy. The girls were just dragging one foot back and forth, making a sound like a metal brush. After a while they changed feet.

"Now, Zoe," Miss Lavatier said, "you see what we do?" Zoe nodded. "You try it."

Miss Lavatier started the music again. Zoe brushed, standing on one foot. The foot began to wiggle. Brush–brush. Her foot wiggled faster. It was like being on one ice skate. Brush–brush. She could feel herself losing balance. All at once she lost it and crashed into Opal Wheeler.

"Well, my gosh! Look out!" Opal said. "You don't have to knock a person down."

"I couldn't help it," Zoe muttered.

The girls began to giggle.

"Never mind, now. Never mind, girls," Miss Lavatier said. "We have to remember this is Zoe's first day."

Zoe caught sight of herself in one of the mirrors. She was blushing. And I'm fat, she thought. And I have straight hair and braces. And I have a scab on my knee. What she was not going to do, though, was cry. She could feel the beginnings of crying in her throat, so she frowned hard and coughed.

"Opal, you take Zoe over by the barre and work with her a few minutes, will you?"

Opal said she would. "All you have to do is brush," she said to Zoe. "Just keep your balance with one foot and brush with the other."

"I know what to do. I just can't *do* it," Zoe said.

"I'd be ashamed to have such a terrible attitude," said Opal.

THE PHANTOM KILLER STRIKES AGAIN

Zoe could see it all in her mind's eye: front-page headlines and a photograph of Opal with an ice pick through her heart. Zoe grinned.

"I don't see what's so funny. If I was the worst dancer in the class I'd feel awful," Opal said.

78

Zoe gritted her teeth. This was the worst experience of her life. She felt like punching Opal and getting out of there. She didn't see what good talking to Opal Wheeler was doing their war work. She'd never have a chance to talk to Miss Lavatier with all this going on.

"If I'm nice enough to stand here and help you, you should at least try," Opal said.

"O.K., Opal." Zoe balanced on one foot and started brush–brushing. She did better. She guessed hating Opal helped her balance.

"Now girls, join the group. We'll combine the brush–brushes with a step-two-step," Miss Lavatier called.

Miss Lavatier demonstrated this step twice. When she did it, it looked easy. Really she was pretty graceful for someone so old. Zoe tried it. Brush–brush, step-two-step. She glimpsed herself in the mirror. She looked like a hippopotamus.

"Now with music!" They all tried. The tune was "The Red, Red Robin."

She's ruined that song for me forever, Zoe thought. She was panting.

"Excuse me a moment, girls," Miss Lavatier said. "Keep practicing the same thing."

Zoe glanced up from her feet. Standing in the changing-room door was Mr. Pear! Zoe's heart bounced. He had on the same wrinkled gray suit. He was wiping his forehead with a handkerchief.

Zoe half expected to see Joe Bunch come creeping up behind. He swore that he never let Mr. Pear out of his sight except at night. Well, he'd missed it this time. This was evidence! Zoe was excited.

Miss Lavatier walked into the changing room and said something to Mr. Pear. It was impossible to hear them. The music was loud and they were talking quietly. Zoe tried to move forward a little with each brush–brush. The line of girls wasn't exactly straight, anyway. She worked forward slowly, hoping she looked as though she couldn't help it, wobbling more than she really had to.

When she was about five feet from the changing room the music stopped. The record continued turning and scratching. The girls stopped tapping. Miss Lavatier turned toward them, then back to Mr. Pear. "Tonight, then," Zoe heard Mr. Pear say.

"After nine o'clock?" Miss Lavatier asked. She looked nervous. She kept wetting her lips and glancing behind her.

"After nine. Your house," Mr. Pear replied.

Zoe bent over to look at her scab. She knew from experience that her face looked guilty when she felt guilty. When she looked up Mr. Pear was gone. Miss Lavatier was changing the record.

After nine o'clock, Zoe thought. After nine o'clock tonight. She wanted to be sure to remember exactly. This was important. She stared at Miss Lavatier. There was nothing about her that looked like an enemy agent. On the other hand, she didn't look exactly normal either. Miss Lavatier had dyed hair for one thing. You could tell because most of it was orange, but the part nearest her scalp was mouse-colored. She was skinny in a way. Her legs were skinny, her neck was skinny, but her stomach stuck out. She had the kind of figure that if she were your mother you'd wish she wouldn't wear a bathing suit. At least around your friends.

So maybe that's how an enemy agent looks, Zoe thought. Maybe she has scars you can't see.

She realized she had been staring at Miss Lavatier. Now Miss Lavatier was staring at her. "Wool-gathering, Zoe?" Miss Lavatier said.

"What?"

"You'll notice everyone else is in line."

Zoe noticed this was true. Opal Wheeler was looking disgusted. "I'm sorry," Zoe said.

"Once more through the brush–brush, step-two-steps, and then, I'm afraid, we'll have to stop for today."

Miss Lavatier started the music. The girls began dancing. Zoe struggled. She could hardly wait to tell Joe Bunch what she'd overheard. It made the whole morning worthwhile. She hardly minded the dancing. Accidentally she jostled Opal.

"Move over!" Opal hissed.

The record ended. "All right, girls, I'll see you next Saturday," said Miss Lavatier. "Zoe, you stay after a minute, will you?"

Zoe had been glaring at Opal when she heard her name. "What did you say, Miss Lavatier?"

"I asked you to stay after a minute."

The other girls flocked off into the changing room. Miss Lavatier was replacing records in a metal rack. Zoe had a creepy feeling. She wondered whether somehow Miss Lavatier knew what she was up to. Maybe she knew Zoe had overheard her conversation with Mr. Pear. "I'm in a pretty big hurry, Miss Lavatier," she said.

"It will take just a minute." Miss Lavatier smiled. She went to the door of the changing room. "Everyone try to remember all her belongings today," she said.

What'll take just a minute? Zoe wondered. Why's she waiting for the others to leave? A thought flickered at the edge of her mind. Joe Bunch had mentioned torture. Of course that was silly. That was just typical Joe Bunch. Still—Zoe swallowed. Her throat felt dry.

"Now." Miss Lavatier turned back to Zoe. Zoe heard the last girls go out the door. "I thought you did very nicely today."

"Thank you." Zoe tried to smile. Surely Miss Lavatier wasn't keeping her after class to say *that*!

"And I know it isn't easy to come into the class late."

"No." Zoe glanced quickly behind her. She had had the sudden feeling that someone might be sneaking up behind her with an ax.

"So I thought perhaps I could give you a little extra help. If you stopped by my house a few times—"

Zoe swallowed. She didn't know what to say.

"It wouldn't take long to catch up to the others."

Zoe nodded. Her heart sank. *Extra* lessons! But she knew it was her best chance to get to know Miss Lavatier. It's my duty, she thought grimly. I'll have to do it. Miss Lavatier took Zoe's arm and smiled. She looked kind of embarrassed. "You know, Zoe, I want to confess that when I was your age *my* secret ambition was to be a dancer, too. I wanted to be a ballerina."

Zoe nodded. She studied the toe of her tap shoe. Why on earth was Miss Lavatier telling her this?

"I worked hard at it for years. I studied for a while with a small group in Chicago. It was lovely." Miss Lavatier looked dreamy. She seemed almost to be talking to herself. "It was just lovely," she repeated.

Suddenly she shrugged. She let go of Zoe's arm. "Well, anyway, here I am now. Things happen, one thing and another. And I do enjoy teaching.

"But I know about secret ambitions, Zoe. They're very important." Zoe nodded. "And don't worry, dear, we can have you dancing as well as the others in no time."

"Thanks, Miss Lavatier," Zoe said. "I'll certainly keep that in mind."

"Fine." Miss Lavatier watched while Zoe changed into her sneakers. "Late any afternoon," she said.

"O.K. Thanks, Miss Lavatier. I'll stop by," Zoe said. She grabbed her paper bag. She ran down the stairs, past the dentist's office, and out the front door. She could see weeks and weeks of extra lessons ahead. "I ought to get a Purple Heart for this," she muttered.

(8)

Across the street, in the doorway of the Turcotte Bakery, Zoe saw Joe Bunch. He pretended not to notice her. She crossed the street and stood at the bakery window, studying a plate of sugar cookies. Joe cleared his throat and started off up the street toward the square. Zoe looked at the cookies long enough to give him a head start and then she followed. She knew Joe well enough to know that this was what she was supposed to do.

She caught up with him in front of the shoe-repair shop. "What took you so long?" Joe said crossly. "Everybody else left a long time ago."

"I was getting to know Miss Lavatier. Isn't that the whole idea?"

Joe kicked a stone into the gutter, then gave her an approving look. "Hey, wait!" He dodged into the alley between the shoe-repair shop and the bank. "Tin can," he explained, returning with an empty number 2 tomato can. "Some people don't know there's a war on."

"But listen, Joe! The main thing is Mr. Pear was there. He came in during class and talked to Miss Lavatier."

"I know that," Joe said. "Rosie and I trailed him all the way from the station. That's why I was waiting for you."

"I wondered why you were acting so mysterious."

Joe ignored her. "What did they say?" he asked.

"I couldn't hear much. I heard Mr. Pear say, 'Tonight?' Then Miss Lavatier said, 'After nine o'clock?' and Mr. Pear said, 'Sure.' So I guess something's going to happen after nine tonight."

"Boy," said Joe, "I wish I knew where."

"Oh—at her house. That's the other thing he said."

Joe nodded. "We'll have to be there."

"How can we? That's past our bedtime."

"Zoe, this is war work. Do you think our soldiers worry about their bedtime?"

"What about my mother, though? She worries."

"O.K.," said Joe, "if you don't want to take chances, you shouldn't be doing war work."

Zoe groaned. It wasn't enough to be taking extra tap-dancing lessons. Having to stand Opal Wheeler every Saturday morning forever was nothing, she supposed. A person could hate Joe Bunch if she thought about it.

"All right, all right," she said crossly. "Where's Rosie?"

"Trailing Mr. Pear."

"Rosie! But, Joe, that's *crazy!* She's much too little. That's dangerous!"

"Everybody's got to do something, Zoe. There's not enough of us to be everywhere."

"Well, that's the dumbest thing I ever heard of.

We'll have to go right after her. She isn't even allowed to cross Main Street."

They had reached the edge of the square. "Come on," Zoe said, "crossing the square is quickest." She began to run. Fang came wheezing along behind. Joe sprinted by her just to prove he was still faster. They came out of the square in front of the Queenie.

Mr. Bunch was out on the sidewalk inspecting a rip in the Queenie's orange-and-green awning. "Quick, down the alley!" Joe whispered, but Mr. Bunch had seen them.

"Look at that!" he called, pointing at his awning. "Slashed! Can you beat it?"

Neither Joe nor Zoe knew what he meant. Mr. Bunch was always grumbling about something. "What happened, Dad? How'd the awning get torn?" Joe asked.

"Torn, nothing!" Mr. Bunch shouted, "Slashed! One of those damned racketeers. That's what!"

Zoe looked at the awning. There was a long ragged cut in the canvas. Someone had cut Mr. Bunch's awning? She couldn't imagine anyone being so brave. "Maybe the wind ripped it, Mr. Bunch."

"Wind? What wind? Hasn't been a breath of a breeze for two weeks. It was racketeers, I tell you. Ever since the War started and they built that bomber plant in town, nothing's the same. Honest man has to fear for his life, that's what." He slapped the scalloped edge of the awning. "Come on in and I'll give you a phosphate," he said.

86

Mr. Bunch never gave anyone anything. Zoe could see that this was a serious occasion. Then she remembered Rosie. "I have to find my sister, Mr. Bunch."

"Rosie? I saw her go by a while ago. She was walking along chatting with John Pear of all people, talking a mile a minute."

Zoe looked at Joe, but he was looking up at the awning. He was no use when his father was around. He got very quiet and so polite it was sickening. "I think I'd better go find her, Mr. Bunch," Zoe said. "It's nearly lunchtime."

"Maybe another time," Mr. Bunch said absently. He went on fingering his ripped awning and muttering to himself.

Zoe wondered whether Joe would follow her. "Well, bye!" she said loudly.

"You go along with Zoe," Mr. Bunch said. "It isn't safe to be alone in this town any more."

When they were out of sight of the Queenie Zoe said, "What was Rosie doing talking to Mr. Pear?"

"How would I know?" Joe said absently.

"Well, it worries me."

"She's all right," Joe said. "She's so little nobody would think she was a spy."

"But—"

Joe wasn't listening.

"What did your father mean—racketeers?" Zoe persisted.

"Oh, he thinks everything is racketeers," Joe said

impatiently. "It's because of the black market. See, the black market is full of racketeers. They get meat and tires and other stuff that's rationed and sell it illegally for a lot of money."

"What does your father mean then?"

"I guess he's just nervous about them. Every time something goes wrong he says it's racketeers. See, if anyone gives these racketeers any trouble they do something terrible to that person. Shoot him usually. I mean if you don't buy their stuff or something, they kill you. It makes my father nervous."

"Does he buy their stuff?"

"Oh, Zoe, he doesn't even know any of them. He's just nervous. You know my father."

"Well, there *was* a cut in his awning."

They were passing the ten-cent store. Joe stopped and glanced behind him. He looked solemn, maybe even scared. "You don't think that was racketeers!" he whispered. "That was a *sign* as sure I ever saw one."

"Of what?"

"Why, a sign the Enemy knows we're on his trail!"

"You mean enemy agents did that?" Zoe felt hollow from the back of her throat to the bottom of her stomach. "You think an enemy agent cut the awning?"

"Of course I do."

"But why would anyone cut the Queenie awning if they wanted to scare *us*?"

"Well, they know the Queenie belongs to my father, for one thing."

88

Zoe stopped and looked at Joe. "You mean the Enemy knows about *you?* You mean they've found out what we're doing?" She gulped. "And who we *are?*"

"They must know about me anyway."

"But, Joe, nobody's even seen us. I mean nobody was around when we read the note and that's the only possible time—"

"Mr. Pear's seen me," Joe said quietly.

"Oh." Zoe didn't know what to say. She looked back in the direction of the Queenie. She could see the raw cut edge of the awning flapping. "Oh, Joe," she said, "aren't you scared?"

Joe shrugged, but his face looked funny. "Maybe a little," he said.

"Well, let's just stop. Let's mind our own business starting right now."

"That's up to you. Personally I wouldn't let my country down that way."

"But if they know we're after them, they'll be after us! Joe, it's dangerous!"

"We'll change our strategy. I'll stop going to the station. I may be the only one they suspect so far. They'll think I've given up. We'll fool them."

Zoe nodded. She wished she could be brave. She knew it was a flaw in her character. Right now, when she wanted more than anything to prove her courage to Joe, she couldn't even talk.

The railroad station was just ahead at the end of the block. "You'll have to go in alone," Joe said. "I don't want Mr. Pear to see us together." Zoe nodded again.

"O.K.," she croaked.

If it hadn't been for Rosie she would have turned around and run home that minute. She longed for her nice safe house and her nice safe mother and Bernice, who could beat up anybody. "Go on," Joe said.

Zoe started toward the station, looking straight ahead. She felt as though enemy eyes were peeking at her from behind every doorway. If they know about Joe, they may know about me, she thought. Then: Of course they know about me! Why else was Mr. Pear at Miss Lavatier's studio? He was warning her, that's what! Zoe bit her lips to keep them from trembling. Her paper bag was rattling against her leg like a castanet.

And that's why she wants me to come to her house. And that's why I could overhear what they said. They wanted me to overhear! They want Joe and me to be sure to be there tonight.

She had almost reached the station. She glanced back and saw Joe waiting a block away. She had a feeling he knew all this, too. He had already figured it out. He just doesn't want to scare me, she thought. For a minute she almost loved Joe Bunch.

Now she understood why Miss Lavatier had been so nice to her. Secret ambitions, hah! Miss Lavatier just wanted to be sure that if they didn't catch them tonight they'd get a second chance. Zoe shuddered. The first time I came for extra help she would—Zoe didn't want to think about it, but she guessed it was obvious enough. The first time she went to Miss Lavatier's house, they'd kill her! Zoe gritted her teeth. She had reached the station.

There were a few people waiting on the platform for the 12:01. Mostly they were men in Army uniforms. At least somebody will hear if I have to scream for help, Zoe thought. She gathered her courage and pushed open the station door. Inside the station it was so gloomy that for a minute she couldn't see anything. Then she saw Mr. Pear, sitting behind the ticket window. He was wearing a green celluloid eyeshade. Right next to him, sitting on a tall stool, was Rosie.

"Hi, Zoe!" Rosie was grinning. "Mr. Pear, this is my sister, Zoe," she said.

Zoe nodded. She didn't trust her voice. "How do you do?" Mr. Pear said. "Rosie has been helping me sort tickets."

Joe is probably right about Rosie, Zoe thought. She's so little no one suspects her. Over Mr. Pear's head was a clock that said five minutes to twelve. Under it was a calendar that said July 3. Zoe leaned against the door for support. Why, tomorrow is the Fourth of July! she thought, but she was too nervous even to enjoy thinking about it.

"We have to go home for lunch," she said to Rosie.

"First," said Rosie, "I have to tie my shoes."

While Zoe waited for Rosie, she looked around the

station. There were big War posters on the walls. One said, "Uncle Sam Needs *You!*" That was to encourage people to enlist in the Army. There was another one with a picture of a huge ear on it. It said, "Sshh—The Enemy May Be Listening." Zoe had never seen that one before. She stared at it. Then she felt her hair begin to prickle. The Enemy was right behind her! When she turned around, Mr. Pear was looking at her.

He knows I know, she thought. It made her feel weak. "Come on," she said to Rosie. "We're going to be late." Her voice came out in a croak. She wondered whether Mr. Pear had noticed.

"O.K." Rosie stood up. "Thanks, Mr. Pear. I had a lot of fun with you."

"Come again, Rosie, any time."

Rosie grinned her steam-shovel grin. She patted her doll in her back pocket. All Zoe wanted was to get out of there fast. She shoved Rosie forward toward the door. "Stop pushing me," Rosie said. "I'm hurrying."

"Just get moving," Zoe hissed under her breath. She pushed Rosie through the door onto the platform and grabbed her hand. They left the station just as the noon whistle began to blow.

(9)

All the way up the street Joe asked Rosie questions. "What did he *say?* I need to know exactly what he said."

"Mr. Pear has had a very sad life," said Rosie. "I feel sorry for him."

"I don't feel sorry for him," Zoe said. "You should have seen how he was staring at me in the station."

"When he was nine his dog died. It was an Irish setter. Also, he gave me some bubble gum." Rosie reached into her pocket and fished our four pieces of bubble gum. It was the good kind.

"Four pieces!" Joe said. "Where would Mr. Pear get that?"

"Your father was selling it this morning, for one thing," Zoe said, remembering the line outside the Queenie.

"No, he wasn't. That was a false alarm. He thought he was getting some, but something happened. He's never sure when he's getting it."

Rosie began replacing the gum in her pocket. "I'm going to save it for a very special day," she said.

Zoe knew better than to ask for any. Rosie had a

stubborn streak. Maybe sometime she'd offer a piece, but she'd never give you any if you asked. "I wonder if it would be safe to chew that gum," Zoe said.

"Poison, you mean." Joe nodded. "That's good thinking, Zoe."

"If you think you're going to get my gum that way, you're wrong," Rosie said. "I know what you're trying to do."

"Oh, Rosie, don't be such a baby!" Zoe said. "We have more important things to worry about than getting your bubble gum."

"Can't fool me." Rosie was trying to look dignified and intelligent.

"The thing is, Rosie, Mr. Pear is an enemy agent," Joe said patiently. "And we think he has suspicions about our work. So Zoe's right. Maybe that gum is poisoned. To get rid of one of us, see?"

Zoe looked sideways at Joe. He knew all right!

"I don't think Mr. Pear is any enemy agent," Rosie said. "He's a nice man and he wouldn't poison gum."

"Maybe it's got nerve paralyzer in it," Joe said thoughtfully.

"If he isn't an enemy agent, what was he doing at the apple tree, Rosie? You saw him yourself. You're the one who knew him!"

"I think he might have a brother," Rosie said, "who looks just like him from a distance."

Joe groaned. "See?" Zoe said. "She's impossible."

"Well, he *could* have a brother," Rosie said. "You two never believe anything I say."

They had reached the corner by the Queenie. The sound of the noon whistle was dying in the air.

"What we could do," Joe said, "is let my father analyze a piece of gum. Then we'd know if it was safe for Rosie."

"Wouldn't he think that was kind of strange?" Zoe said. "He'd wonder why we thought the gum was poisoned."

"Well, we'd have to lie a little. Come on. You don't even have to talk. I'll do it all."

Joe led them through the front door of the drugstore. It was dim inside and cool, the damp kind of cool that reminded Zoe of museums. The store smelled of vanilla and iodine. There was a big wooden fan on the ceiling that looked like an airplane propeller. On one side of the store was a soda fountain. On the other side was a long dusty glass case full of Whitman's Samplers and hot-water bottles. Mr. Bunch had moved the magazine rack back near the pharmacy where he could keep an eye on the comics. The pharmacy, at the back of the store, was really all Mr. Bunch cared about. His beakers and bottles were polished and gleaming while the rest of the store stayed dusty. He had rows of them lined up on the shelves that partitioned the pharmacy from the rest of the store.

Coming in from the sunlight, Zoe couldn't see for a minute. She stood blindly blinking, sniffing the vanilla–iodine smell. The odor was like the noon whistle. It had been there for as long as Zoe could remember. She liked it.

"Why are you just standing there?"

Zoe had forgotten all about Rosie. "I was thinking," she said. "Where's Joe?"

"He went in back to find his father."

"Did you give him a piece of your gum?"

"Half. He told me to stay out here so I wouldn't hear him lying."

That was just like Joe Bunch. He didn't mind lying himself blue, as long as he didn't have an audience who knew better. Zoe could understand that. It ruined the realism to know there was someone around who didn't believe you.

She walked over to the display case and studied the hot-water bottles and perfume. There was an advertisement for Tabu cologne propped in the case. It showed a man holding a violin about to kiss a lady at a piano. The lady was half standing up and half sitting down. It looked uncomfortable. She's getting ravished, Zoe thought. This was a word Zoe had seen in certain books that she read under her bed with a flashlight. Heroines often got ravished in these books, but Zoe had never been sure what that looked like. It looks like doing a backbend, she thought.

Rosie was sitting on a stack of magazines, reading an Archie comic. Mr. Bunch must be analyzing the gum, Zoe thought. Nothing else could take so long. In that case it was probably safe to read a few comics. She began looking through the stacks on the magazine rack for new ones. Something made her turn, a sudden feeling that someone was watching her.

She looked around, and there, crouched down between a packing case and the pharmacy wall, was Joe Bunch! Zoe was about to say something. Then she stopped. Joe's finger was on his lips. With the other hand he beckoned her. Zoe crept across to where he was hiding. "What—" she began.

"Ssh! Listen!" Joe whispered.

Zoe listened. She could hear two voices coming from the storeroom behind the pharmacy. She recognized one of them as Mr. Bunch's. She'd never heard the other one before. "I told you *no* once. I'm telling you *no* again," Mr. Bunch was saying softly. "Don't think you're going to scare me into it."

"The awning was just a little reminder that you'd better keep your lip buttoned," the other voice said.

"Don't use your scare tactics on me, sir." Mr. Bunch began to talk louder. "There're laws, you know. I can get legal protection."

"I wouldn't do that, Mr. Bunch, if I was you."

"Don't you threaten me!" Mr. Bunch said.

"Call it a warning, Mr. Bunch. Just say you've been warned."

Zoe looked at Joe. His eyes were enormous. They heard the back door open and close. "Let's get out of here!" Joe whispered. They scrambled up and dodged around the magazine rack.

"Come on, Rosie!" Zoe said.

For once Rosie didn't argue. She dropped the Archie comic and followed them. Zoe didn't look back to see where Mr. Bunch was. She and Rosie followed Joe headlong out the front door.

"Come on," Joe whispered. "We've got to follow that man, whoever he is. It's the guy who slashed the awning and he's threatening my father because of us!"

They ran around the side of the building. The back door of the store opened into the alley behind the Queenie. The three of them crept along the side wall to the alley. Then Joe crouched down behind the Queenie trash cans and peered carefully around them. Zoe looked, too. A hundred yards down the alley she saw a man walking away. He wore a white straw hat and white summer shoes!

"Miss Lavatier's boyfriend!" Zoe gasped.

"Let's go," Joe whispered.

"He'll see us!"

"Not if we're careful," Joe said. "Follow me."

The alley was long. Behind every store were rows of trash cans, cardboard boxes, wooden crates. Joe ran, crouched, from the Queenie trash cans to a crate behind Pickard's shoe store. Zoe and Rosie followed. They wedged themselves between the crate and the wall and watched while the man passed behind the dry-goods store. He did not look back. He walked steadily, not seeming to hurry. Behind the Sun Bonnet Dairy he stopped to light a cigarette.

"What'll we do when we catch him?" Zoe whispered.

"I don't *want* to catch him," Joe said. "I just want

to have a look at his face. And I want to see where he's going. The thing is I don't want him to see us."

The man began walking again. Joe squeezed out from behind the crate and ran forward, keeping close to the wall. He dropped down behind a trash can outside the dry-goods store. Zoe held her breath and followed him. She had a superstition, left over from when she was little, that if she held her breath, Time stopped. Nothing could happen to her until she breathed again. She dropped down beside Joe and took a deep breath. They crowded together to make room for Rosie.

"He'll be out of the alley in a minute," Joe whispered. "Watch which way he turns. I'm going to duck through Mrs. Perch's and beat him to the corner. That way he won't know I followed him. If he turns the other way, follow him until I catch up with you."

Before Zoe could answer, Joe was crawling toward the door of Mrs. Perch's knitting shop. She watched him try the door handle. Mr. Bunch kept the Queenie's alley door locked, but Mrs. Perch's door was open. Joe turned the handle slowly. Then he eased the door open a crack at a time. Zoe and Rosie watched breathlessly. Rosie was chewing her doll's pigtail.

When Joe had the door open wide enough to slip through sideways, he turned back to Zoe and Rosie. "Watch *him*, not me," he hissed and disappeared into the knitting shop.

Zoe was just turning around again to peep over the trash cans when she heard an awful crash. It seemed to come from inside Mrs. Perch's shop.

100

"What was *that?*" Rosie said. Zoe shook her head. She didn't know whether to run or to freeze behind the trash can. There was a lot more rattling and crashing and then raised voices. Joe came hurtling out the door of the shop.

"Run!" he cried.

(10)

"Which way?" Zoe shouted. But Joe was already pounding down the alley in the direction the man had taken. Zoe and Rosie jumped up and followed him. Rosie caught a trash can with her foot and sent it clattering down the alley ahead of them, spreading paper and bottles as it turned.

Zoe ran. She watched her feet running. She didn't dare look forward or back. Ahead was the Enemy and probably certain death. Behind was some other catastrophe she didn't even understand. This was by far the worst of all Joe's schemes. "If I ever get out of this alive, I'll never do anything like it again, God," she prayed. She gritted her teeth and kept running.

She could hear Rosie's feet pounding along behind her. Farther back she could hear a shrill old voice that must belong to Mrs. Perch screeching Joe Bunch's name. Even farther back she could hear Mr. Bunch bellowing. Zoe just kept watching her feet running. They began to seem strange, at first like someone else's feet and then not like feet at all. She was hypnotized by these strange blue objects moving back and forth, back and forth over cinders and dirt, black and brown. Cinders and dirt, cinders and dirt, back and forth, blue and brown and then, suddenly, *plop!*

Zoe had run straight into something soft. It grunted. Zoe fell to the ground. She felt pain in her knee. "Ouch!" she cried and opened her eyes. The first thing she saw, right before her face, was a pair of white summer shoes.

"Oh, no!" Zoe whimpered and closed her eyes.

So this is the way it ends, she thought, stabbed to death in an alley at the age of eleven. She lay still, waiting for the final moment. She wondered whether it would be a blow or a shot.

Instead, a voice said, "Are you all right, honey?"

Zoe knew it was a trick, but she looked up. She looked straight into the eyes of Miss Lavatier's boyfriend. "I think I skinned my knee," she said.

"You were really flying. Your pals went by me like bullets. Guess you didn't see me."

Zoe shook her head. He *seemed* nice, but it was all a plot, of course. He was the Enemy. He just wanted as much information as he could get before he killed her. Zoe gritted her teeth. He wouldn't get any. She would protect Joe and Rosie until death.

BODY OF YOUNG GIRL
DISCOVERED BEHIND MOVIE THEATER
Suspect Enemy Agents Involved

Her eyes filled with tears as she pictured the headline.

She could see her mother in a black mourning veil receiving a medal from the President. The flags were at half-mast. The medal said something about bravery beyond the call of duty.

"Hey, don't cry." The man knelt beside her in the alley and pulled a handkerchief from his pocket. "Let's see your knee," he said.

Zoe sat up obediently. She bowed her head and looked at her shoes. This was the moment. She was proud of how bravely she faced it. "What you want to do is run home, and wash that knee," the man said. "It's full of cinders. Here." Zoe looked up. He was unfolding his handkerchief. He wound the handkerchief around her bloody knee and tied it securely. "Now then, run on home and have your mother wash it," he said.

Zoe looked at him suspiciously. She couldn't believe he wasn't going to murder her. "Thank you, sir," she said quietly. He smiled. He looked something like a spy all right, but he had a nice smile and one gold tooth. Zoe had never thought about spies going to the dentist, but, of course, they must.

"I should have said 'walk,'" the man said. "You seem to get into trouble running."

Zoe gave him a shaky smile. She guessed he really was going to let her go this time. He would save murdering her for when she got to Miss Lavatier's.

I almost like him in spite of that, Zoe thought. He really was nice. If he hadn't been an enemy agent, who was planning to kill her, he'd have made a nice friend.

She stood up and brushed off her shorts. She picked up her bag of shoes and glanced behind her. The alley was empty. Mr. Bunch and Mrs. Perch had disappeared. "Well, thanks again," she said. "I've got to get going." He nodded and his gold tooth flashed.

She hurried to the end of the alley and turned the corner. The man did not follow her. Even now she half expected to feel a bullet hit her between the shoulder blades but when she turned to look back, the man was bent over dusting the knees of his trousers.

Her own knee was beginning to sting badly. She started to walk the five blocks home. She began to get angry at Joe and Rosie for leaving her. She might be brave, but they certainly weren't. An experience like this separates the sheep from the goats, she thought grimly.

She walked stiff-legged because of the handkerchief around her knee. It was hard to believe that a man who'd put his own handkerchief around someone's bloody knee could be a dangerous enemy spy. Still, Zoe knew it was true. It was the same with Mr. Pear. Rosie thought he was a nice man. He'd given her bubble gum. But all three of them had seen Mr. Pear take the note from the apple tree. It was hard to understand. In the movies bad people were bad and good people were good. It was simpler that way.

Zoe walked slowly. She was worn out. She was so late for lunch now that it didn't really matter whether she hurried or not. Bernice could scold herself hoarse for all Zoe cared. She walked along swinging her shoe bag.

She thought she could feel her knee oozing blood with every step. "Joe Bunch can do his own stupid war work," she muttered. "Maybe all those people *are* enemy spies. So what? Joe Bunch doesn't even know what they're spying on. He'll probably never find out either. It'll end up like the diamond rings."

She had reached the corner of Underwood and Happy Hollow. An orange butterfly flew up from the sidewalk ahead of her and fluttered into the vacant lot. That's one place I won't go again, Zoe thought. Stinky old sumac. She thought she saw something move at the edge of the sumac patch. She watched. Sure enough, Fang came waddling out into the sunshine, wagging his tail. So Joe and Rosie were hiding in the sumac. That was wonderful of them—running off and hiding at the first sign of danger—really wonderful.

Zoe stood with her hands on her hips and stared at the sumac patch. She knew they were watching for her. In a minute Rosie's face peeped out between the branches, then Joe's. They both looked pale and scared. Zoe didn't move. She stood and watched them hurry toward her.

"Are you all right?" Joe said. He looked really frightened.

"Oh, Zoe, I was so scared for you!" said Rosie.

Zoe just looked at them.

"What happened to your knee? Whose handkerchief?" Joe asked.

"I fell down. I've got cinders and blood all over my

knee. That dangerous enemy agent tied it up with his handkerchief."

"Well, good grief, Zoe! Take it off! It's probably poisoned. There's probably poison seeping into your veins right now!"

"Don't be dumb, Joe. I'm tired of your stupid games. I suppose that man carries poison handkerchiefs in his pocket just in case somebody happens to fall down?"

"Anything's possible, Zoe. This is serious business."

"Not any more, it's not. Not with me. I'm quitting before I get killed," Zoe said.

Rosie stood there nodding. It was hard to tell whose side she was on. Suddenly she pointed down the street behind them and began stuttering. "Look! Help!" Joe whirled around.

"Oh boy! Let's beat it!" he said and headed for the sumac patch. Zoe couldn't see anything so terrifying— just Mr. Bunch and Mrs. Perch walking up the street talking—but she followed Rosie and Joe.

"One more complication and I'll have a nervous breakdown!" Joe said, peering out from the sumac branches.

Zoe sniffed and fingered her sore knee.

"See, what happened," Joe said, "is that when I was sneaking through Mrs. Perch's, I knocked over some brooms and buckets and stuff. They fell onto a glass case full of yarn. Just one little part of the glass broke though." He sighed. "Mrs. Perch must have gone after my father."

Mrs. Perch and Mr. Bunch were even with the vacant

lot by now. Mrs. Perch was talking a lot and waving her arms. Mr. Bunch was nodding. He looked tired.

"I'll definitely have to run away from home now," Joe said.

"What do you mean 'run away'?" said Zoe.

"Why if I went home now I'd get locked up for the rest of the summer. Between that guy threatening my father and what just happened down at Mrs. Perch's, I'm done for."

"So where will you go?"

"I don't know. Doesn't matter. Someplace far away, I guess."

"You can hide out here and I'll bring you lunch," Rosie said.

Joe shook his head. He stared at his feet. "It wouldn't matter so much except for the war work. I know we were about to uncover something big."

Zoe looked at Joe suspiciously. She'd heard him threaten to run away plenty of times before. "Maybe you wouldn't get locked up," she said.

"Hah!" Joe sighed. "If we could have been at Miss Lavatier's tonight like we planned, I know we'd have cracked this spy ring."

"We'd have been killed you mean!" Zoe was really mad. "You know as well as I do they planned the whole thing so they could get both of us down there and kill us!"

Joe looked funny. "I didn't think you'd figured that out yet," he said.

"Of course I have! But what I'm wondering is why you didn't tell me. You were just going to let me walk into a trap!"

"Well, I didn't plan to let them catch us! I thought we could hide somewhere and watch. It's my life, too, after all!"

"So why didn't you tell me? Why did you pretend they didn't know about me?"

Joe looked solemnly at the branches overhead. "I wanted to spare you, Zoe," he said. "I didn't want to worry you."

Zoe sniffed. In a way, that was very nice of Joe if it was true. She didn't know what to say.

"Doesn't matter now, though," Joe said. "We'll never know what we might have found. You're quitting and I'm forced to leave town." He sighed deeply.

"Oh, shut up, Joe!" Zoe said. "I won't quit." She suspected she'd been tricked. She wondered why she never learned. It irritated her.

Joe looked up. "Thanks, Zoe. You're a wonderful friend," he said.

"Oh, well." Zoe hoped she wouldn't blush, but she could feel her cheeks getting warm.

Rosie was squirming beside them. "I'm so hungry. Couldn't we go home for lunch?" she asked.

"You two go on," said Joe. "Don't worry about me."

"Well, I'm not going to," Zoe said. "You weren't exactly dying of worry over me, I noticed."

All the way home she was mad at Joe Bunch. I'm too

111

nice to him, she thought. He takes terrible advantage of me.

Bernice was mad, too. She had their sandwiches wrapped in waxed paper in the refrigerator. "You two ought to be spanked," she said. "One hour late. If your mother was home she'd take her slipper to you."

"For your information, Bernice, I was in a serious accident. I have to wash my knee," Zoe said.

"Let's see," said Bernice. "I'll wash it." But Zoe was already halfway upstairs. She would rather be scalped than let Bernice wash a cut. Bernice washed cuts the same way she washed floors.

Upstairs she ran a little water over her knee and brushed out the loosest cinders. She didn't know what to do with the bloody handkerchief. She knew it shouldn't be washed in case it was covered with enemy fingerprints. Finally she decided to hide it between her mattress and box spring for safekeeping.

They ate their sandwiches at the kitchen table. While Bernice wasn't looking, Rosie stuffed half of hers into her pocket. "For Joe!" she whispered. Zoe chewed slowly and ate every bite. She was already doing plenty for Joe Bunch. She drank all her Ovaltine, too, and hoped Joe was thirsty.

After lunch Rosie insisted on taking the sandwich-half to the sumac patch. Zoe went with her, feeling full and sleepy. The vacant lot was so quiet they could hear grasshoppers whirring in the weeds. The sumac patch was deserted. Joe wasn't at headquarters or anyplace else around. "Joe must have run away out of town already," Rosie said.

"Phooey," said Zoe, "that was all just a trick to keep me from quitting." She kicked a rock and it hurt her toe. "Darn him," she said. "You watch, Rosie, I bet he'll turn up at our house before dinner."

(11)

Zoe and Rosie were sitting on the porch steps waiting for their father to come home. They took turns fanning themselves with a paper fan. Bernice was clattering plates in the kitchen. Their mother was reading the newspaper. It was Rosie's turn with the fan. Zoe picked a leaf from the weigela bush and traced its veins with her thumbnail. "We're having wilted-lettuce salad," she said.

"P.U.," said Rosie. "It seems like we have that every night." Zoe nodded. She didn't like it either. She hated the way the lettuce got transparent and lay like old skin on the salad plate.

"Did Bernice invent it, do you think?" Rosie said.

"Probably. She loves it."

"People's taste gets terrible when they get old. When I get old I'm going to remember wilted lettuce tastes horrible."

Zoe felt her knee tenderly. She pressed the weigela leaf against the scrape. It felt cool and soothing. There were still a few black cinders under the skin. "I thought for sure that Joe Bunch would come over before dinner with some big story about why he didn't run away," she said. "I guess he's embarrassed to see us."

"Maybe he ran away."

"No. He's just a big exaggerator. He'd never do it."

"I think he ran away. I think he went to Chicago and tomorrow he'll go to the Field Museum all day and see the stuffed cavemen."

It was no use arguing. Rosie was too much of a dope. "My turn on the fan," Zoe said.

"When I'm old I'm going to live in Chicago," Rosie said, "and have a long dress completely covered with diamonds."

"I thought you were going to live in New York and be a famous radio star."

"There's radios everywhere," Rosie said. "Hey, look, there's Mr. Bunch!"

Mr. Bunch's old green Ford was coming slowly up the street. Rosie waved. The car rattled up to the curb and Mr. Bunch leaned out. "You girls seen Joe?" he called. They shook their heads.

"No, we haven't, Mr. Bunch," Rosie called, "but—" Zoe poked her leg.

"Let me talk," she whispered. "Don't you say a thing."

"Well, he's missing," Mr. Bunch called. "He hasn't been home since morning."

Zoe stood up and started down the sidewalk. She was thinking what to say. She didn't want to tell Mr. Bunch Joe had run away. Even if he had, she hated to tattle.

Still, Mr. Bunch looked so tired and old and worried that she felt sorry for him.

"I saw him at noon, Mr. Bunch."

"So did a lot of people. He was breaking up Mrs. Perch's display case at noon."

"I saw him after that, over by the vacant lot." Zoe could have bitten her tongue. Now what if Mr. Bunch went prowling through the sumac patch and found his binoculars?

"Didn't say where he was going?"

"No, he didn't. He didn't say where he was going at all." Zoe felt pleased with herself. She wouldn't call that a lie exactly.

Rosie stood beside the car with her lips pressed together so firmly they were turning white. Anyone who knew Rosie even a little bit would know she had a secret. Her throat was twitching like a bag of frogs. Any minute she'd start talking. "Rosie, you go ask Mama if she's seen Joe," Zoe said.

"But we know—" Rosie sputtered.

"Don't bother your mother," Mr. Bunch said. "He'll turn up, I expect. When he does I'll have a few things to say to him." Mr. Bunch roared the engine. "Here I am using gasoline! I haven't enough gas to drive across town and I use it looking for him!" The motor roared again and a cloud of blue smoke belched out the exhaust pipe.

Poor Joe, Zoe thought. She could see why he was scared to go home. Rosie coughed and waved her arms. They were standing in a cloud of blue fumes. Through the haze Zoe could see her father's old Packard chugging up the street. Nobody's car worked well any more. There were no new cars because of the War and the old ones were falling apart.

Her father pulled into the driveway. "Hi-hi," he said. "How are you, Harry?" When her father didn't like someone he said "Hi" to them twice, Zoe had noticed. He couldn't stand Mr. Bunch.

"Worried," Mr. Bunch said. "One thing and another, it's getting so a man can't live in this town."

"It's a bad time," her father agreed. "They're having trouble out at the plant, too." Their father ran a clinic at the bomber plant twice a week. He sewed up people who riveted their fingers, things like that.

"Trouble?" Mr. Bunch looked interested.

"Oh, they're talking about sabotage. They've had a lot of foul-ups in the production line. Personally, I think it's War jitters. Everyone read that piece in the paper about a spy ring, so now they think they're being sabotaged."

Rosie nudged Zoe. Zoe looked at her and made a face which, she hoped, would keep Rosie quiet.

"I don't know about spies," Mr. Bunch said. "Could be the racketeers have something to do with it."

Their father grunted. "War hysteria."

"Maybe yes, maybe no," Mr. Bunch said. "I'd never count out racketeers. Anyway, here I sit wasting gas, and I've got to find Joe."

"Lost Joe?" their father said.

Mr. Bunch nodded abruptly.

117

"Better get him in before dark. Blackout tonight, you know."

"Oh, drat!" Mr. Bunch said. "I forgot that." He jammed the car into gear and it jumped away from the curb in another cloud of fumes.

"Harry's burning oil," their father said thoughtfully. They all watched Mr. Bunch bounce and rattle to the corner before they turned toward the house.

"Is there a blackout tonight, really?" Zoe asked. She loved blackouts, but they didn't happen often. Zoe thought they were the best part of the War.

During blackouts every light in town was turned off so that if any enemy planes flew over wanting to drop bombs the town would be invisible. Of course, enemy planes never really flew over. Blackouts were just practice, like fire drills.

When the noon whistle blew on blackout nights the streetlights went out. Next you'd see one house after another go dark. Cars were supposed to drive without headlights and the stores around the square had to turn off their signs. Pretty soon it was so dark all over that an enemy plane would never have been able to tell where the country stopped and the town began.

Blackouts were scary in a nice way. They weren't too scary because you knew they weren't real. Being in a blackout was like listening to a ghost story. You knew nothing bad would really happen, but if you had a good imagination you could get goose pimples.

"I love blackouts when they don't drop bombs," Rosie said.

118

"What do you mean, 'when they don't.' They *never* do," Zoe said crossly. Rosie was trying to get attention as usual.

"I don't love them," their father said. "Foolish waste of time." Zoe couldn't see why her father felt that way. She thought blackouts were thrilling.

"Your mother won't remember there's a blackout and she'll be cross," their father said.

"Probably Bernice reminded her," said Zoe. "Bernice loves blackouts and air raids and all that."

Their mother was sitting in the living room reading the newspaper. "Zoe, if you've seen Joe Bunch, call his mother," she said. "She's worried he's lost. And, girls, go wash your hands. We want to have a quick dinner so Bernice can finish the dishes before dark."

Rosie was already on her way upstairs to warm up the radio. Zoe trailed after her, feeling hot and out of sorts. She was worried about Joe but she hated to admit it. Joe had threatened to run away lots of times. He'd never done it. Not really. Once he'd run away and climbed a big pine tree across the street from his house. He'd sat there until dark watching his parents look for him. Zoe was sure Mr. Bunch had checked the pine tree this time.

She wandered into her room and sat on the edge of the bed. She wished she'd never agreed to keep on with the war work. If Joe Bunch shows up before bedtime, I'll quit, she thought. Nothing he says will change my mind. But if he doesn't show up—Zoe sighed. There was no way out then. She'd agreed. Joe was counting on her.

119

The thing was, she wasn't sure what to do. She had to be at Miss Lavatier's by nine o'clock, but then what? When she got really honest, she had to admit that Joe was the brains and she was the worrier, the fuss-budget, the scaredy-cat. She scowled at her dancing shoes lying in the corner where she'd thrown them. Even Rosie had more courage. Maybe that was because Rosie didn't know any better. Still, there she'd been, sitting beside Mr. Pear, all alone. Would I do that? Zoe wondered. Of course not. I'd get giant hives and faint.

She looked at her knees. If her father saw her cut knee, he'd want to pick all the cinders out. It would hurt. I wonder if I leave the cinders in whether I'll get gangrene, Zoe thought. I might. I might have to have my leg amputated above the knee.

She could see herself going to school in the fall with an artificial leg. Mr. Pointer, the principal, would stop her in the hall. "You've shown great bravery in the face of trouble, Zoe. You're an example to the whole school. We want to name the library after you."

"Oh, stop it!" Zoe said out loud. "Bravery! You can't even stand having the cinders picked out!"

"Why are you screaming at yourself?" Rosie was standing in the doorway. Her face was shining clean. She had on a dress.

"None of your business."

"Well, dinner's ready and you aren't even clean yet."

Zoe went into the bathroom to wash her face. She looked at herself in the mirror. "Well, I'm not going to be a coward any more," she said. "A person can change. I'm going right down to Miss Lavatier's tonight and get the evidence. I won't even think about how they're plotting to kill me. I'll just do it and that's that." She dried her hands. "Unless, of course, Joe Bunch shows up," she added.

Dinner had begun when Zoe reached the table. Rosie was eating quietly, sitting straight with one hand in her lap. Zoe slid into her chair before anyone could notice her knee. Their father was talking about something. She didn't bother to listen until she heard him say "sabotage." She'd been meaning to ask what that meant.

"Well, it *could* be sabotage at the plant," their mother said. "You read that article in the paper."

"If you read the paper you think there's an enemy spy behind every lilac bush."

Rosie looked up, wide-eyed. "Don't scare the children," their mother said.

"Couldn't there be enemy spies at the plant?" Zoe asked. "One time you said there could be some in town." She hoped she sounded casual.

"Oh, I don't know," her father said. "There could be, I suppose. But just because a couple of nuts and bolts come loose at the bomber plant doesn't mean spies are at work."

Zoe finished her dinner in silence. She ate almost all her wilted lettuce without noticing. The more she heard, the likelier it seemed that Joe Bunch was right. They were on to something big.

After dinner she went out onto the porch to think. She'd better have a plan for tonight just in case Joe didn't show up. She pulled a splinter from the porch step and twirled it between her fingers. Getting down to Miss Lavatier's wouldn't be easy. By nine o'clock it would be dark, the blackout would have begun. She felt faint when she thought about creeping down there in the dark. I just won't think about it any more than I have to, she decided.

The sky had turned the pale gray color of twilight. Zoe could hear her mother closing curtains in the living room. All the curtains in old Mrs. Nutt's house were already closed. At least Mr. Powell was still digging crabgrass. That made Zoe feel a little better.

I'll have to pretend to go to bed, she thought. Probably I can sneak down the back stairs after Bernice is out of the kitchen.

But what if they lock the back door before I get home? Zoe wondered. She knew of a cellar window that didn't lock. It's a long drop to the floor, she thought, but I did it once. She tried to remember whether you pushed or pulled to open the window. Then she thought of something else. What if the warden who checked to be sure everyone's lights were out mistook her for a burglar and shot her?

CHILD SHOT ENTERING OWN HOME
Warden Very Sorry

I have to stop this imagining, Zoe thought. It's my worst habit.

From far away across town came the faint howl of a train whistle. Oh, boy, Zoe thought, that must be the 8:10 train coming in. Only fifty minutes to go.

Rosie put her head out the screen door. "We have to be in bed before the blackout starts," she said.

Zoe stood up and took one more long look at Victoria Street. There wasn't a sign of Joe.

"We have to get ready for *bed!*" Rosie repeated.

Ordinarily Zoe would have told Rosie to mind her own business. Tonight she hadn't the heart. She took one last look toward Joe's house, then brushed past Rosie into the hall.

(12)

Zoe put on the only pair of pajamas she had that fit. If I have to spy in pajamas, at least my stomach won't show, she thought. She didn't feel well organized. Except for the sneaking-out part, Zoe realized she didn't begin to have a plan. Strategy was what she needed and she was terrible at strategy. She wasn't sure what she was expected to do. Watch, she guessed, and listen. It was hard to know what to watch when you didn't know what you were looking for. I'll just get close to the house and hide, she decided. What I do next will depend on what happens.

She wondered whether she needed a weapon. She kept her father's old fish knife in the top drawer of her dresser. It wasn't very sharp, but it had a point that could pierce a person's heart. I'd better take it, she thought.

She wrapped the knife in a handkerchief Mrs. Nutt had given her for Christmas. Then she put it under her pillow. She put her sneakers together beside her bed where she could find them in the dark.

Her mother was going from room to room upstairs turning off lights. "Better get into bed, girls. It'll be dark in a few minutes," she called. Zoe looked at the clock in the hall. Eight thirty-five. She felt doomed. She climbed into bed and pulled up the sheet. She fingered the knife under her pillow. She could hear faint music from Bernice's room. The back stairs would be safe, then. She heard her mother going downstairs. It must be nearly a quarter to nine, she thought. She lay still, listening. Her parents were in the living room. They could have a lamp on in there if they closed the door, because of the heavy blackout curtains that kept light from showing outside.

Zoe sat up and felt for her sneakers. One of the laces was in a knot. "I'll just have to go barefoot," she muttered. She picked up the knife. She tiptoed to her bedroom door and listened. The house was dark. She stole to the top of the stairs and looked down. The living-room door was closed. Only a pencil of light showed underneath. Well, O.K., she thought. This is it.

She crept into the back hall, past Bernice's room to the top of the back stairs. Bernice was listening to the radio. Zoe could hear the announcer's voice. "Lucky Strike Green has gone to War," he said. She felt for the banister. The back stairs creaked, but if she leaned most of her weight on the rail going down they didn't creak badly. She went slowly, a step at a time, stopping to listen. She heard her mother cough. Another step, then another. She couldn't see a thing. She knew Bernice kept a broom on the bottom step. She'd have to miss stepping on that. After each step she felt ahead cautiously for the next one. I must be near the bottom, she thought. She groped for the broom. She felt it just ahead. The banister ended. She was in the downstairs hall.

Zoe stopped there to listen and to catch her breath. She was as breathless as if she'd run all the way to school. She clutched the knife tighter and crept forward. The screen door showed before her, a lighter patch of dark. The door was locked and Zoe fumbled up and down its side, trying to remember where the lock was. She felt the hook and pushed it up, standing on her tiptoes. It stuck. She pushed harder. The hook swung free and Zoe almost fell through the screen. She stopped and held her breath. Somebody surely had heard her! She waited. There was no sound but the hum of Bernice's radio. She pushed open the screen door.

It was lighter outside. Zoe tiptoed through the wet grass behind the Victory garden. It seemed queer to see all the houses dark. It was as though the whole neighborhood had gone away on vacation at once. She decided not to risk the sidewalk or the alley behind the house, although they would be easier going. Instead she crept through the back yard and into the yard next door, keeping close to bushes.

Her feet were wet. She could hear a sprinkler in the grass, but she couldn't see it. Suddenly a gust of cold water hit her face like a slap. She almost screamed. Her pajama top was sopped. She shivered. "I'm not going to cry," she said. "That was just a sprinkler." All the same, she sniffled a little as she ran along the row of lilac bushes into the next yard.

Someplace nearby a dog began barking. He smells me, Zoe thought. What if he's a bloodhound? She stopped to listen. The dog kept barking, but he was across the street. "No use worrying," she muttered.

There was a fence between the next two back yards, but Zoe knew where there was a hole big enough to squeeze through. She felt along the fence until she came to the gap. Carefully she eased herself between the broken pickets, feet first. Ahead, just one house away now, was Miss Lavatier's yard.

Suddenly Zoe trembled. Creeping through the backyards, she'd almost forgotten what she was doing. Now, all at once, she was terrified. She could see Miss Lavatier's house, dimly white in the darkness. She had to get around the side of it to someplace near the front-porch steps. Otherwise she might not see whatever it was she'd come to watch. She held tight to her knife and crept forward.

When she got to the edge of Miss Lavatier's yard, she noticed a hedge running along beside the driveway next to the house. She ran to it and dropped to her knees. She crawled along between the hedge and the house until she was almost around the side. The hedge ended beside the front porch.

But where can I hide? Zoe thought. She looked around, squinting in the darkness. Then she saw that under Miss Lavatier's porch there was a crawl space just like the one under her own. Her father used their crawl space to store the garden hose. Rosie and Zoe used it for hide-and-seek. There would be plenty of room to hide under there if she could find an opening. She felt along the wooden lattice that hid the crawl space until her hand came to a piece of the lattice that wiggled. It was exactly like the one at home. She tugged and the lattice came open enough to let her crawl in.

She felt inside. The floor of the crawl space was packed dirt. There was enough room to allow her to sit up if she wanted. She shivered. She knew crawl spaces were full of spider webs and bugs. She wiggled through the hole as quietly as she could, holding her wet pajamas close to her so they wouldn't catch on the lattice. Carefully, she pulled the lattice closed. Then she turned and tried to see where she was. It was as black as a bottle of ink inside. She put out her hand to feel around. Suddenly, she gasped. She had touched somebody!

(13)

Zoe jumped back and froze against the lattice. She had touched somebody's face! She had felt warm skin and part of a nose. Somebody was here in the crawl space with her!

Her breath jerked. Her heart banged. I've got to get out! she thought. She groped along the lattice with one hand, trying to find the piece that wiggled. She wasn't even certain she was against the right wall. She'd jumped and she wasn't sure in which direction.

She stared into the darkness. Whoever it was must be nearby. The crawl space was not very big. But she could see nothing. Outside near the porch, a cricket was chirping. Between chirps Zoe listened. She thought she could hear somebody breathing.

She had to escape! She groped along the lattice as far as she could reach. It all seemed solid. Carefully she inched forward on her knees a little at a time, feeling for the opening. She could hear the breathing not far away. Whoever it was was waiting for her to make a move. She had to be careful. Stealthily she crept forward another inch and felt along the lattice. Another inch.

All at once, something moved directly in front of her. She lost her balance. She teetered. She toppled onto something warm. A fur coat!

The fur coat growled.

Bears! Zoe thought. Bloodhounds!

Then the fur began to wiggle and pant. Zoe felt a rough tongue licking her face. "Fang?" she whispered. The animal wriggled all over, making happy noises.

"Zoe?" She heard her name hissed from the far end of the crawl space.

"Joe?" she whispered. She felt like crying with relief. Fang was covering her face with wet licks. She sat up and held him in her arms. "Where are you?"

"I'm coming." She could hear Joe creeping toward her. When he got close she could just make out the outline of his body, a blacker bit of darkness.

"What are you doing in here?" Suddenly she was furious with him.

"Spying, of course."

"Well of all dumb things! I thought you ran away." Joe Bunch was awful. He was the worst boy she'd ever known, leaving her to do the spying and then turning up at the last minute and scaring her to death.

"I did run away. I went to a movie. Then when it got dark I came over here."

"Well, that's the stupidest thing I ever heard. Why didn't you run far away?"

"War work," Joe said. "I decided that a person doesn't leave his duties because of a little danger."

"I told you I'd do it."

"Well, I thought you might not. I thought maybe you'd get scared as usual."

Zoe grunted and for some reason her eyes filled with tears. Darn Joe! She was glad it was dark so he couldn't see her. "Well, maybe you would have," Joe said.

"I'm here, aren't I?"

"You kind of scared me creeping in here. I didn't know *who* it was."

"I told you I'd be here. I keep my word," Zoe said, "which is more than I can say for a big liar like you."

"Liar? What do you mean by that?"

"Running away! Some running away from home this is!"

"I'm not home. And I'm not going home. I never said I was going to Alaska or anything."

"Well you better go home, Joe. Your mother and father are worried."

"Yes? Well, *I'm* worried, too. My father'll kill me after what happened at Mrs. Perch's, added on to what that guy must have told him in the Queenie."

Zoe nodded. Probably that was true. Mr. Bunch was terrible when he got mad.

"Well, as long as you're here, I'm going home," she said.

"What do you mean 'going home'? You promised me you wouldn't quit! Anyway nothing's happened yet!"

"I'm going home before it does. I promised myself I'd quit as soon as I laid eyes on you again. Joe, I think these *are* enemy agents and I think it's way too dangerous for us."

"Sssh," Joe said. "Hold onto Fang."

Zoe did as she was told. She heard the sound of a car turning into Miss Lavatier's driveway. The tires crunched on gravel. The brakes squeaked gently. It stopped beside the porch, just even with the crawl space.

They heard the car door open quietly. They heard someone come out on the porch overhead, then someone else going up the steps. Zoe could feel Fang's body begin to vibrate. "Fang's going to bark," she whispered.

"Hold his mouth shut tight," Joe said.

From above them came the sound of voices. Whoever it was, was talking too quietly for Zoe to make out the words. There was a deep murmur that sounded like a man's voice and a higher one that she thought must belong to Miss Lavatier. Then there seemed to be a third voice, another man's low rumble. Zoe wished she could see Joe's face. "Can you hear what they're saying?" she whispered. Joe didn't answer.

Fang began squirming in her arms. He growled softly, deep in his throat. Zoe held his mouth closed with all her strength. If Fang barked now, she and Joe might as well commit suicide.

The voices overhead stopped. Footsteps crossed the porch. Then there were steps coming down to the driveway again. The car door opened with a crack. Something jingled—car keys probably. There were more steps coming down.

132

Zoe reached out to touch Joe. He was not there.

"Joe!" she whispered.

"Over here."

She crawled toward Joe's voice, dragging Fang along by his muzzle. Joe was leaning against the wooden lattice trying to see outside. Zoe squatted beside him. They must be right next to the car, she thought. She could hear feet on the gravel nearby.

"Look," Joe whispered. "It's a truck."

Zoe squinted through a square of the lattice. Outside the crawl space it was lighter. She could see three figures standing beside a small truck. One of them was Miss Lavatier, all right. The other two were men.

"Give me a hand with the stuff," one of the men said. "Lillian, you open up for us."

The man who had spoken walked around to the back of the truck. Zoe could see him outlined against the sky. The other man followed. When they reached the back, Zoe saw that the first man was Mr. Pear. The second one wore a white straw hat and white summer shoes.

Mr. Pear and Miss Lavatier's boyfriend began lifting cartons out of the truck. They were about the size of Coca-Cola cases, but twice as tall. "What's in them, do you think?" Zoe whispered. Joe nudged her to be quiet. The men lifted the cartons as though they didn't weigh much. Mr. Pear stood holding several of them in his arms.

All at once there was a rattling noise not three feet

from where Zoe was crouching. She started and almost let go of Fang. Joe's hand was on her shoulder. "Move over here," he whispered. She squirmed toward him. Fang was vibrating from head to tail. He was dying to bark.

Zoe strained her eyes in the direction of the noise. Someone was pulling open the gate in the lattice that she had climbed through!

(14)

"They heard us!" she whispered. "Oh, Joe, they're after us!" Joe clapped his hand over her mouth.

"Be *quiet*," he whispered directly into her ear. It made her furious to have Joe holding her mouth shut as if she were as undependable as Fang. But she was too frightened to move.

"I've opened the crawl space," she heard Miss Lavatier say.

"All right, Lillian. Here, give us a hand." Zoe thought that the man who had spoken was Mr. Pear, but she couldn't be sure.

There was a grunt outside the lattice, then a head poked through the opening. I wish I could faint, Zoe thought. I wish I could turn invisible. She and Fang were shaking so much, she was sure they were making noise.

"Hand me a couple," the head said. There was a rustling sound. Something was shoved across the dirt floor. It almost touched Zoe's knee. She reached out gingerly and felt the object beside her. It was a cardboard carton. They were loading the cartons into the crawl space!

Another grunt and somebody shoved another stack of cartons in. "Better hurry it up," a voice said. "The lights will be coming on any time." The cartons started to come faster. Zoe began to feel squeezed. She nudged Joe to move over. As quietly as they could, they crept farther into the corner.

They were being walled in with cardboard boxes. Zoe guessed there must be fifteen or twenty of them at least. She could count seven within her reach. How would they get out? She remembered hearing about the Black Hole of Calcutta where people had been so crowded they just died. We'll be skeletons by the time anyone finds us, she thought.

"O.K., that's all of them," a voice said.

Zoe could hear the lattice door scratching shut. The voices grew fainter. Then there were footsteps above them again and the sound of the screen door closing. "Let's get out of here, if we can," Zoe said.

"No, wait. It isn't safe. They might come out again."

"Then you hold Fang." Fang was wriggling in her arms. He was trying to get at the boxes, sniffing and growling under his breath. "What do you suppose is in all these boxes?" Zoe said.

"I don't know. Explosives probably."

"Explosives!" Zoe had thought of guns or maybe bayonets—but explosives! "We better get out of here, Joe. They could blow up. We could be blown to pieces!"

Joe sighed. "Explosives don't blow up by themselves, Zoe. You have to light them. Boy, I wish I had a flashlight! I'd like to examine these boxes. They might say *Caution* or *High Explosives* or something. Then we'd have positive proof."

"Oh, yes. I'm sure the Enemy marks all explosive boxes like that. Sometimes you're as dumb as Rosie, Joe. Do you think they'd be so careful hiding these in the dark during a blackout and all if they were going to have *Explosives* printed right on the boxes?"

"If we had a flashlight we could maybe make a little hole in the cardboard and see in."

"Yes, and start everything exploding."

Zoe was huddled as far from the cartons as she could get, but she knew it was no use. There were enough boxes of explosives in the crawl space to blow up the whole town. "Don't let Fang chew anything," she said.

"Quiet," said Joe. The screen door opened overhead. A light flashed and disappeared. Heavy steps came down the porch stairs.

Then it was quiet. Zoe had a feeling someone was standing right outside the crawl space listening for sounds. She was afraid to breathe. After a few minutes she smelled cigar smoke. Then she heard a cough. Someone must be sitting on the steps smoking, she thought. Her legs ached from being cramped in one position. Her foot itched. She shifted her weight as quietly as she could. She began to think Joe had fallen asleep, he was so quiet. She poked his knee and, after a moment, he poked her back.

Then, all at once, it seemed to grow lighter in the

crawl space. Zoe peeped through the lattice. The streetlights were on. "Joe," she whispered, "the blackout's
over! I have to get home!" At the same time she heard
steps on the porch.

"All right, John, let's go," a voice said.

Zoe peered out. She saw both men. Mr. Pear was still
wearing his wrinkled suit. Miss Lavatier's boyfriend
was halfway into the truck. The truck's engine rumbled
and the headlights came on. Zoe was blinded by the
sudden glare. The truck backed slowly out the driveway.
The lights swung sideways out of her eyes and Zoe
watched the truck move off down the street.

"Darn. I wanted to get the license number," Joe
whispered. They listened for another minute to make
sure Miss Lavatier had gone inside. Then Zoe said, "I've
got to go right now. My parents will be going to bed
and they'll miss me."

"O.K.," Joe said, "but let's just take one little look at
these cartons first."

The cartons were all around them. Zoe couldn't see
any way to get out except to squeeze over the top between the porch floor and the carton lids. Rosie would
have fit all right, but Zoe was worried about her stomach.

"If only I had my flashlight," Joe said. "It's still too
dark in here to see much."

"Well, I'm leaving. It'll take forever to get out."

"What we'll do is come back tomorrow night with a
flashlight," Joe said.

"I don't know," Zoe said. "I'll think about it."

140

Right then she just wanted to get home. She could worry about everything else later. She crawled along the stacks of cartons looking for a way out. Between the cartons and the wall of the crawl space she found a narrow slit. By sucking in her stomach and holding her breath she thought she could squeeze through. She wedged herself into the crack and struggled along. She was going to make it, she could see, but it was going to be a lot of work.

Joe caught up with her at the gate in the lattice. "So be ready tomorrow night. Plan on meeting me around nine again," he said.

"Where are you going?" Zoe was panting. "You're not going home, are you?"

"I guess maybe I will. I think it's going to rain. Otherwise I definitely wouldn't. I'd sleep at headquarters."

"Then come over in the morning and we'll talk about plans."

"Probably I'll be staying home in the morning," Joe said.

"Oh, your father you mean. I bet you won't get out for a week, Joe."

"I can sneak out at night. And like I say, I wouldn't go home at all except for the rain."

"Come *on*. I have to hurry."

Joe shoved at the lattice door and it came open with a scratching noise. They crawled out. Joe eased the door back into place. "Well, O.K.," he whispered. "See you tomorrow night." He went off toward Victoria Street with Fang loping behind. Zoe started toward her house, taking the back way again.

There were lights on all over the neighborhood, so that she could go faster. She hurried. She squirmed through the fence and ran along the row of lilac bushes in the next yard. The same dog was barking. Somebody had turned off the sprinkler. She could see it gleaming faintly in the light from the house as she ran into her own back yard.

She stopped near the back fence to study the lights in her house. The kitchen light was on. That was bad. She could see lights in the living room. Her mother must have opened the blackout curtains. While she watched, someone snapped off the kitchen light. She crept along the edge of the Victory garden, past the rosebed, up to the back steps. She paused to listen. It was quiet. She tiptoed up the steps. The screen door was still unlocked. Boy, am I lucky! she thought.

She eased the screen open enough to step through. She could hear her mother and father talking in the living room. They sounded normal. Good! she thought. They haven't missed me. She hurried up the back stairs. It didn't matter now if she made some noise. She could always say she was getting a drink of water.

The upstairs hall was dark and quiet. Bernice was probably asleep. Zoe could hear Rosie snoring lightly. She tiptoed into her room. I ought to change my pajamas, she thought. But they had dried long ago and she was sleepy. She looked out the window and remembered the next day was the Fourth of July. I've had so much on my mind I've forgotten the good things, she thought.

The sky was bright with stars. Stars! "I thought Joe Bunch said it was going to rain," she said as she got into bed.

(15)

When Zoe woke she knew it must be early. A mourning dove was sitting on the telephone wire outside her window making its sad throbbing sound. The air felt damp. She lay still for a while, thinking things over. She was pleased with herself for going down to Miss Lavatier's alone the night before. It showed she was getting braver.

Zoe stretched and yawned. She was sure that they had almost enough evidence to call the police. Their part of the work was nearly over. She guessed she'd spend the rest of the summer working on journalism or maybe writing a novel.

Zoe had been thinking about writing a novel since she was seven. She had started one once, but she'd finished the whole plot in five pages. I think this time I'll write one about a beautiful nurse who falls in love with a man who gets killed in the War, she decided. She'll find him dying on the battlefield at the end. Zoe could see her bending over to hear his last words in the sunset. Bullets and bombs would be exploding all around them. The nurse's raven black hair would be blowing out behind her.

Zoe sniffed. She was almost in tears. Her own stories always made her cry, especially the endings. She was good at endings. She was pretty good at beginnings. It was in the middle part that she got stuck.

From someplace outside there came a bang. The Fourth of July! Zoe sat up in bed. She was almost sorry the day had arrived. She hadn't had time to look forward to it. How did anyone happen to have a firecracker? Her father had said there were no fireworks because of the War. "Black market," Zoe muttered. She wished the black market weren't so illegal. It was the only place that had a lot of the things she liked best.

She heard Bernice clumping down the back stairs. She jumped out of bed and ran to the back hall. "Happy Fourth of July, Bernice," she called down the stairwell. Bernice looked up at her and squinted her eyes.

"What have you got all over you?" she asked. "It looks like mud."

"Mud?" Zoe said vaguely, but immediately she knew what was wrong.

"Didn't you take a bath last night or what?" Bernice asked.

"The blackout, remember? We didn't have time."

"Well, you're up awful early." Bernice was always grouchy in the morning.

Zoe ran to look in the mirror. She didn't feel dirty, but she saw that her face was streaked with mud. There were spider webs in her hair. Her good pajamas were covered with dirt and grass stains. It's a good thing Bernice is nearsighted, Zoe thought.

She pulled off her pajamas and rolled them into a ball. She didn't dare throw them down the clothes chute. She looked around her room for a hiding place. Finally, she stuffed them between her mattress and box spring.

She went into the bathroom and put the stopper in the tub. While the tub filled she pulled spider webs out of her hair. It made her shiver to think of the spiders that had probably been hanging in the crawl space in the dark. I'm more afraid of spiders than enemy agents, she thought. How dumb.

Zoe stepped into the tub and washed fast. The water turned from light to dark gray. One of her eyes smarted from the soap. Zoe closed it and sloshed water onto her face. When she opened her eyes Rosie was standing in the doorway. "Why are you taking a bath in the morning?" Rosie said.

"Is there some law against it?" Zoe pulled out the stopper and reached for a towel.

"This is the Fourth of July."

Zoe said nothing.

"You were dirty!" Rosie said. "Remember, our relatives are coming for a picnic," she added.

"But no parade this year. No fireworks," Zoe said sadly.

"How did you get so dirty? Last night you weren't."

Zoe hadn't decided whether to tell Rosie about being under Miss Lavatier's porch. She was afraid that Rosie was already keeping about as many secrets as she could. "How did you?" Rosie insisted.

"None of your business." Zoe wrapped the towel

around her and pushed past her sister. Rosie followed her into her bedroom.

"If you don't tell me, I'll tell Mama you were all filthy."

Zoe sighed. It was no use. Rosie would tell and then there would be trouble. Rosie probably had a right to know anyway, since she'd been in on the rest of it. "I was under Miss Lavatier's porch. Joe and I were. We were spying."

"So Joe didn't run away?"

"Well, not really. Anyway, we saw them unloading cartons from a truck. They put the cartons under the porch, almost right on top of us."

"Who?"

"Joe and me."

"No. Who was putting them under the porch?"

"Oh. Mr. Pear and Miss Lavatier and Miss Lavatier's boyfriend. Joe thinks the boxes are full of dynamite."

Rosie nodded. Zoe couldn't tell whether she understood or not. Maybe she hadn't heard of dynamite. "Explosives, Rosie. Joe thinks they're full of stuff that blows up buildings."

"Like TNT," Rosie said. She looked thoughtful. "I was under Miss Lavatier's porch once."

"When?"

"Oh, once. With Gracie. When we were playing kick-the-can."

"You never said you were under there."

"I was, though. It was awful under there. Did you see the coal chute?"

"I couldn't see anything. It was dark, remember?"

"There's this door under there that goes right into the cellar. Gracie said it was where they put coal for the furnace. We looked in. You can see the cellar perfectly."

"It isn't locked?"

"Nope. It's just like our clothes chute. No locks."

Zoe opened her dresser drawer. "That's a secret, Rosie, about last night."

"Well, I know it. Tonight I want to go, too."

"What do you mean 'tonight'?"

"Aren't you going again?"

Zoe groaned. She wondered how it was to be an only child. Perfect, she bet.

"So can I go?"

"O.K., Rosie. If we go, you can go," Zoe said reluctantly. It was no use. Rosie would keep insisting until she got her way.

After breakfast Zoe stood in the kitchen and watched Bernice fry chicken for the picnic. Bernice was in a hurry. She had the day off after she got the picnic ready. She was planning to go down to the USO and dance with the servicemen, she said. The USO was a kind of club for soldiers in the baggage room next to the train station. Soldiers who had long waits between trains could go there to dance and have Cokes. Zoe couldn't imagine why any soldier would want to dance with Bernice but she didn't say so.

Bernice was very skinny. She wore Chen-Yu nail polish—a color called Dragon's Blood—and she had a mustache. Still, Bernice was a good cook and Zoe liked watching her.

"Does Norbert mind if you go to the USO while he's overseas?" Zoe asked.

Bernice jumped out of the way of a splatter of hot grease. "Of course not. It's my patriotic duty to entertain our soldiers," she said. She lifted the pan of chicken off the fire.

They always had chicken at family picnics, also potato salad, and sliced tomatoes. The children had lemonade, the grownups had bourbon. Their grandmother usually brought a spice cake and a bouquet of zinnias. Zoe felt happy. She liked every single person in her family. She planned to be nice to all of them.

The telephone in the front hall rang. Zoe could hear Rosie answering it. "Zoe!" Rosie called. "Telephone!" Zoe was surprised. She hardly ever got phone calls. She hurried into the hall. Rosie was holding the receiver. "I can't tell who it is!" she whispered, pressing the mouthpiece against her chest. "It's a funny voice."

Zoe took the receiver. "Hello," she said. For a minute nobody answered. "Hello," she said again.

"Zoe?" The voice was a whisper.

"Yes. Talk. I can't hear you."

"It's me. Joe."

"What's wrong with your voice?"

"I'm home. I can't talk. I'm not allowed to use the phone. Can you meet me at headquarters?"

"Now?"

"Ten minutes."

"I guess so."

"Bring some glue." There was a click.

"Joe? He's hung up."

"That was Joe?" Rosie said. "I think he needs his tonsils out."

"That's the way he whispers," Zoe said. "He never learned how to do it right."

"Was he telling you about *tonight?*" Rosie mouthed the last word silently.

"No. I have to meet him at headquarters."

"I'm coming."

"All right. Just go and get the glue."

Zoe had given up trying to lose Rosie.

(16)

They walked side by side toward Victoria Street. When they got near Miss Lavatier's house they could see Miss Lavatier out in front watering her dahlias. Just as though last night never happened, Zoe thought.

"Let's cross the street," she whispered to Rosie, but Miss Lavatier had already seen them.

"Good morning, girls!" she called. She was smiling.

Zoe tried to smile. She was sure her face looked funny.

"I'm giving my flowers a drink. We haven't had rain for so long."

Rosie stopped. "Your roses are beautiful, Miss Lavatier."

"Actually they're dahlias, dear. But perhaps they do look a little bit like roses."

Zoe nudged Rosie to keep walking. Rosie didn't budge. "I like the purple one best," she said.

"That's a nice one," Miss Lavatier agreed. She hesitated, then put down the hose. "You may have it if you like it," she said. She took a little pair of scissors from her pocket and cut the purple dahlia. She cut it with a nice long stem.

Rosie grinned. "Thank you," she said. "I'll keep it forever, Miss Lavatier. First I'll keep it in water and then I'll squash it in a book so I'll always have it."

That seemed to please Miss Lavatier. Zoe nudged Rosie to get her going. "What did you do that for?" Zoe hissed when they were out of earshot.

"Well, don't you think it's pretty?" Rosie had stuck the flower in the buttonhole of her shirt.

"Miss Lavatier certainly doesn't know much about kids," Zoe said, feeling cross. "If she did, she'd have given us each a flower."

"I'm going to let you have a piece of my bubble gum," Rosie said.

For a minute Zoe was pleased. Then she was suspicious. "Why?" she said.

"Because you didn't get a flower."

"Oh, no that's not why. It's because you're getting worried about it. You think maybe Mr. Pear *did* poison it."

"There's Opal Wheeler," Rosie said calmly.

Opal was sitting on her front porch holding a small American flag. She had on a white dress, white shoes, and white socks. Her hair was curled. "Ugh," said Zoe.

"Hi!" Opal called. "Are you two going for a walk or what?"

"Don't answer," Zoe said. "Keep walking. She'll want to come along."

"Can't you answer?" Opal called. "Stuck ups!"

"Hi, Opal," said Rosie.

"I'm on my way to my grandmother's in a minute," Opal said. "Then I'm going to a movie and to have a soda."

"Wow," said Zoe.

"How come you're going for a walk? Aren't you having any celebration or what?"

"We're having a picnic," Rosie said.

"So are we. At my grandmother's. Then we're going to a movie and—"

"Then you're having a soda. Well, be seeing you, Opal," Zoe said.

Rosie was standing looking into space. "Come on," Zoe muttered. Rosie looked thoughtful, then she began to smile.

"Opal," she said, "I'm going to give you some bubble gum. Because it's the Fourth of July."

"Gosh," Opal said.

Rosie reached into her pocket and pulled out the gum. She gave Opal all three and a half pieces.

Zoe didn't say a word until they reached the corner. Then she looked sideways at Rosie. The purple dahlia bounced on her chest. She was smiling a little to herself.

"I like candy / I like cake," Zoe chanted softly. Rosie grinned. "There's just one thing / I really hate." Rosie giggled.

"Opal Wheeler!" they shouted together.

"Well, she deserves it," Zoe said. She wondered how long it took the poison to work. She imagined Opal, with her white dress and curly hair, writhing in pain on the porch steps.

"Maybe it isn't really poisoned," said Rosie.

When they arrived at the corner of the vacant lot they could see Fang chasing a butterfly through the weeds. Zoe whistled softly when they reached the edge of the sumac. Joe whistled in reply.

Headquarters was a mess. Joe was lying sprawled on the ground surrounded by magazines and newspapers. Scraps of paper were scattered about him. He was clipping something from a magazine with a large pair of pinking shears.

"Did you sneak out?" Zoe asked.

"Yup. My father's working half a day."

Zoe stepped around a stack of newspapers and looked over Joe's shoulder. "What are you doing?" she said.

"Writing the FBI."

"No. I mean *really*."

"Really," Joe said. "You don't think I'd write them in my own handwriting?"

"I don't get it."

"I decided we have to write the FBI. They should know Miss Lavatier has about a million tons of explosives under her porch."

"You don't know that."

Joe groaned. "Well, what *else* could be in those cartons?" he said.

"Why not call the police then?"

"The FBI's better. They've had more experience

with war and spies and all. I don't think Captain Olsen would believe us if we told him. Anyway, he knows my Dad."

Captain Olsen was the policeman Mr. Bunch called whenever there was trouble at the Queenie. "I guess you're right," Zoe said.

"So I'm cutting out a lot of *a*'s and *b*'s and all from magazines and we can glue them to paper and make words. That way if the letter gets into enemy hands they can't trace it by the handwriting. I've read that's how counterspies do it."

"Should I start gluing?"

"I guess you could glue 'Dear Sirs.' I don't know what else we'll say yet."

"I'll make the envelope," said Rosie.

Zoe squatted down beside Joe and picked through the pile of letters he had cut out.

"You ought to sort these into alphabetical stacks," she said.

She found a *d*. She glued the back of it and stuck it to the sheet of paper near the top. "It's not a capital *d*."

"Doesn't matter." Joe was scissoring carefully, biting his tongue.

"Did your Dad say anything about the threat?" Zoe asked.

"Not a word. I can't figure it out. He had plenty to say about Mrs. Perch."

"Maybe he thinks we got scared by the awning and quit."

"That's what I hope he thinks," Joe said.

"I've got 'Dear Sirs' done. What'll I put next?"

"I'm working it out. I think we'll say: 'Dear Sirs, By sheer accident we have happened upon an enemy spy ring—' "

"Better say 'I' instead of 'we,' to throw them off the track."

"Good. Then say, 'I think that they are going to blow up the bomber plant soon.' "

"Joe, do you really think that?"

"Sure I do. 'And I think—' Maybe you ought to write this down first, then glue it. 'I have found a hidden supply of explosives under Miss Lillian Lavatier's porch. She lives at—' whatever her address is. Then say, 'I do not expect a reward or medal. Yours truly.' "

"Yours truly, what?"

" 'A patriotic American Person.' "

"Oh, that's good, Joe. I don't see how you can make things up in your head that way."

Joe cleared his throat. Joe always cleared his throat when he was pleased or embarrassed.

"Tell me the envelope," Rosie said.

"Just FBI, Washington, D.C."

Zoe handed Rosie the glue while she searched for an *e*. "I think we ought to leave out a few words," she said after a while. "I'll never get all this glued today. What about leaving out 'sheer accident'?"

"I kind of liked that part," Joe said wistfully. "It sounds realistic."

156

"Well, what about the reward and medal part?"

"No. That's important. They might think we were just after money."

"I'm going to leave out 'sheer.' That's two more *e*'s."

"I'll help you," Rosie said. "The envelope's done." She held it up for Zoe to see.

"Rosie, not FIB! FBI, dummy."

Rosie's face fell. Her chin began to tremble.

"Never mind. The glue's still wet. We can fix it."

"Don't tear the envelope. I had to sneak it out of my father's desk," Joe said.

It seemed to Zoe that they had been gluing for hours. The letter looked quite pretty, she thought. The words were all different sizes and colors and, except for a place where a blade of grass had stuck accidentally, it was perfectly glued. She was searching for a *p* to begin *patriotic* when the noon whistle blew.

"Oh, my gosh!" Joe said. "I have to get home. My father's closing the Queenie at noon. If he finds out I sneaked out—" Joe shook his head. "Here's a stamp to mail it when you finish."

He jumped up and began gathering magazines in his arms. "Some of these are new," he explained. "Be at Miss Lavatier's at nine. Bring your flashlight so we'll have an extra."

"I'm supposed to finish this now?" Zoe asked, but Joe was already out of hearing, hurrying through the sumac. "O.K., Rosie, hand me the glue," she said. She felt grouchy.

157

It seemed to her that they'd never finish. They looked and looked for an *s* for *person*.

"Couldn't we use a *z*? I've been saving one just in case," Rosie said.

"It'll look illiterate, but all right," Zoe said. She was tired of the whole project. They folded the letter and put it in the envelope. Rosie pasted on the stamp.

There was a mailbox on the corner of Underwood Street and Oak Street. Zoe let Rosie drop the letter in the slot while she checked the pickup times posted on the front of the box. She was looking forward to the lemonade. She was hot.

They stood on the corner of Victoria Street waiting for a car to go by. As it passed them, Opal Wheeler's head popped out the rear window. "Hi!" she called. "I'm on my way to my grandma's." Then she blew an enormous pink bubble that wavered in the wind before it broke.

Rosie and Zoe looked after the car. "She must be chewing all three and a half pieces," Zoe said.

"And they weren't poison," said Rosie.

In a way Zoe felt relieved. Of course, if the bubble gum had been poisoned, that would have been the evidence they needed. A man who'd give poison bubble gum to a little girl was bad enough to do anything. But the bubble gum hadn't been poisoned. It really had been just a present. Zoe sighed. She wished if these people were going to be dangerous enemy agents they'd act like it.

(17)

Zoe could see her grandfather's car parked in front of the house. Sunlight glinted off the fenders. Her grandfather drove the car only on Sundays, polished it every day, and washed it on Saturdays. That was why his fenders sparkled while everybody else's were rusty or patched with gray plastic.

"I knew we'd be late," Zoe said.

"Grandma and Grandpa are always early," said Rosie.

They cut across the front yard. Their grandmother was sitting on the front porch rocking and fanning herself. "Hi, Grandma," Zoe said. She kissed her grandmother's cheek. It smelled sweet and dusty like a petunia. "I'm going to see if the lemonade's made yet," she added.

She wandered into the house. The hall was cool and dimly green like the inside of an aquarium. Her grandmother's zinnias were on the hall table. Bernice came out of the kitchen in a dotted dress. "I'm going," she said. "Have a nice picnic."

Zoe had a glass of lemonade. Then she went upstairs

to find her mother. Her mother was in her bedroom getting dressed. Zoe liked watching her. She liked best watching her dress for a party, but any time was interesting. "When's everyone else coming?" Zoe said.

Her mother grunted. She was painting her leg with leg paint and she had to concentrate. Stockings were scarce because of the War and mothers painted their legs stocking-color when they ran out. Some mothers drew seams up the backs of their legs with eyebrow pencil as well. "I can hear Aunt Martha in the back yard now," her mother said.

Zoe's father had brought half a dozen canvas folding chairs into the back yard. Her Aunt Martha was already sitting in one of them when Zoe came out. Rosie and their cousin Jim were setting up the croquet wickets. That was a tradition. The children played croquet while the grownups talked. Rosie cheated and they let her do it because she was small. She's getting about old enough to stop it, Zoe thought. Nobody let me cheat when I was almost nine.

She looked toward Miss Lavatier's house. It seemed years since the night before, almost as though she'd dreamed it all. She picked up the rack of croquet mallets and carried it across the grass. Rosie took red, Jim took green, and Zoe took black.

They let Rosie start. She got her ball through the first two wickets, but on her next shot she sent it flying into a honeysuckle bush. "Let me move it out," she said.

"Nope. This year you have to play by the rules," Zoe said.

Rosie began to get red. "You always let me!" she cried.

"Not any more."

"But I'm little!" Rosie whimpered.

Zoe shook her head. "You can start over again, but you can't move it."

"It's not fair!" Rosie screamed and began to cry.

Their father turned around. "Let Rosie take it out, Zoe. After all, she's the youngest," he said.

Rosie stopped crying abruptly and went to collect her ball. Zoe was mad. She turned away and stared in the direction of Miss Lavatier's house. She noticed that Miss Lavatier had come out in the back yard and was watering her rose bushes. Zoe was about to turn away again when she saw the truck in Miss Lavatier's driveway. She stared. She was sure it was the same truck! I have to have a closer look, she thought.

"You two play for a minute. I have to go to the bathroom," she said.

She hurried in the back door, through the house, and onto the front porch. If I stroll past Miss Lavatier's kind of casually maybe I can see something, she thought. She'd have to be quick so she wouldn't be missed.

She walked toward Miss Lavatier's house, bouncing a tiny red jacks ball she had in her pocket. The truck was there, all right. She was sure it was the same one.

As she got closer to the house she began to plan. Nobody was in sight. If she hurried she could sneak down the driveway along the hedge and have a look inside the truck.

It was a gray panel truck. On the side were printed the words:

Graves' Nursery
PLUMVILLE

Zoe didn't pay much attention to that. Anything that obvious was bound to be camouflage. Plumville was a dinky town fifty miles away. If you wanted to throw somebody off the track, printing "Plumville" on your truck would be a good thing to do. I'm getting to think like Joe, she thought. That pleased her. She tip-toed quickly down the driveway until the hedge was between her and the house, then ducked down beside the hedge and waited to make sure she hadn't been noticed. For a minute everything was quiet. A butter-fly settled on the hedge, then flew away. Zoe began to ease herself up slowly. All at once she heard a voice. It was a man's voice and it seemed to be coming from under the porch only a few feet away. Zoe ducked.

"Easy does it," the voice said. There was a thud.

"I said easy!" The man sounded cross. He must have been listening to someone else, for suddenly he said, "I know you don't like it, but there's no other way. Bunch is out."

Zoe gulped. They were talking about Joe! They must have heard about him running away.

"A few days is all I'm asking," the man said. "I'll figure out something else. But I got no place for this load. Most of it's promised at the bomber plant."

162

Zoé couldn't believe it. It was like Joe had seen it all in a crystal ball!

There was another thud. The man swore. "Easy!" he said again, but louder. Zoe recognized his voice then. It was Miss Lavatier's boyfriend, the man in the white straw hat.

"O.K., O.K.," he said, "be reasonable, Lil. At this point we don't want the whole business to explode on us."

Zoe gasped. Explode! She'd heard enough. She was getting out of there. Somehow she had to reach Joe. She *couldn't* wait until nine o'clock. This was an emergency.

She stood up cautiously and peered around the back of the truck. There was still nobody in sight. Good! She turned and ran for home. The evidence was thickening so fast it made her head swim. They were going to blow up the bomber plant! Somehow she had to be sure they didn't make it.

(18)

There was no way to talk to Joe immediately. The picnic was about to start. Aunt Martha and Zoe's mother were carrying food to the table. Zoe's father was cranking the ice-cream freezer. Zoe didn't want to talk to anyone. She wanted to think. But it was no use. She had to get through supper first.

It seemed to her that the picnic would go on forever. She nibbled a drumstick and watched the others. She wondered how she could reach Joe. She didn't dare telephone because Mr. Bunch might answer and she didn't dare go over to his house for the same reason. I'll send him a message by mental telepathy, she decided. She wasn't sure how much to include in the message. Probably something short, like "Call me," was best.

She concentrated. The thing was to concentrate so hard that no other thoughts came into your mind. Call me, Joe, she thought. Call me, Joe. It made her head feel squeezed.

"Zoe, are you in pain?" Her mother really looked worried.

"No, I was thinking." Zoe felt embarrassed.

164

"Are you sure? You were making the most awful face."

"Growing pains," her grandmother said.

Zoe helped her father open the ice-cream freezer. Then she wandered over to the Victory garden and looked at the weeds. She supposed it would be rude to pull weeds during a family picnic, but she was so nervous that that was what she felt like doing. If Joe had gotten her message, he wasn't sending one back. She wondered whether you had to be concentrating to receive messages.

"Zoe, come have dessert," her mother called.

She had to do it or they'd think she was sick. I'm not sure I can even swallow, she thought. She stirred her ice cream and stared at the sky. The sun was low. I wish it would hurry up and set, she thought.

When they had finished clearing the dishes Rosie and Zoe and Jim played Statue. Zoe kept glancing at Miss Lavatier's house and wishing somehow she could contact Joe. After what seemed like about ten years a light went on in the house next door. Finally it's getting dark! Zoe thought.

Rosie and Zoe stood on the front porch with their parents and watched the others drive away. "We get to stay up late tonight, don't we?" Rosie asked.

"Later," their mother said, "for special."

"Let's get up a game of kick-the-can, then," Zoe said. "Come on, Rosie."

"Stay near enough to hear when I call you for bed," their mother said.

Zoe promised. She grabbed Rosie's hand. "Come on!" she muttered.

"How come we're going to play kick-the-can?" Rosie said when they were on the sidewalk. "I thought we were going to Miss Lavatier's tonight."

"We are, stupid!" Zoe said. "We're going right now. I couldn't say that to Mother, could I?"

Zoe wasn't sure what time it was, but it was completely dark and the streetlights were on. "We're going up to Miss Lavatier's and hide in the bushes," she said. "We'll wait for Joe there."

When they got near Miss Lavatier's they crossed the street. Zoe remembered a big snowball bush in the yard opposite where they could hide and wait. The Reams, whose bush it was, were away, so it was safe. Zoe sat down in the shadow of the bush and studied Miss Lavatier's house. Rosie got out her doll and sucked its pigtail. In a few minutes something moved across the street on the sidewalk. Zoe recognized Fang. Creeping along behind him, dodging in and out of the shadows, was Joe Bunch.

"Joe!" Zoe called softly. "Over here!"

Joe stopped and looked around him.

"Over here. At the Reams'," Zoe called.

He understood her. He darted across the street, keeping to his low Indian crouch. Fang galloped along beside and in front of him, almost knocking him down.

"Boy! I almost didn't get out!" Joe gasped, dropping down beside them.

166

"Listen, Joe, you were right about the explosives," Zoe whispered. "I overheard something, and you were right." Zoe told him the story as fast as she could.

Joe looked impressed. She could tell he was pleased, but all he said was, "Are you sure you got the words right? I'll have to put it all in the Spiral when I get home."

"Of course I got it right. I practically memorized it. But, Joe, shouldn't we call someone at the bomber plant to warn them? I mean if they're planning to take explosives out there, someone should be warned right now."

"I've been thinking about that," Joe said. "Somebody'll have to telephone. I guess it'd better be me because of my low voice. Sound more realistic, probably."

"Can you call from home, though?"

Joe sighed and said nothing. Then he bounced upright. "Sure, I can! I'll wait until my father's taking his shower. He takes a shower for about an hour at night and the water makes plenty of noise. I'll call then and he'll never hear me. I'll say something simple like, 'Someone's going to blow up your plant.' No details or anything. Then I'll hang up before they can trace the call."

"Oh, good," said Zoe. "Oh, that relieves me!"

"Well, we'd better hurry," Joe said. "First we'll get another look at those boxes and then I'll go home and call."

Joe tested his flashlight on the palm of his hand.

He looked intently at Miss Lavatier's house. "Looks quiet," he said. "Let's go."

Rosie scrambled up and stuffed her doll into her shorts pocket. "I'm ready," she said gruffly.

They followed Joe across the street. When they reached Miss Lavatier's driveway they kept close to the hedge. Joe stopped to listen. There wasn't a sound from the house. "Quick!" he whispered.

They dashed to the side of the porch and crouched while Joe wiggled open the door to the crawl space. He crawled in first, then Fang, then Rosie and, finally, Zoe. They knelt for a moment, huddled together in the dark, to be sure they hadn't been heard. Then Joe switched on his flashlight.

"They're gone!" Joe gasped.

Joe moved his light slowly across the width of the crawl space. It was empty except for an old wheelbarrow full of garden tools. Joe didn't say a word.

"What shall we do?" Zoe asked.

"Hurry!" Joe said. "They must be on their way to the bomber plant already. I guess they decided not to wait."

"You mean you think they'll blow up the plant tonight?"

"I don't know, but let's go."

They crawled back out into the driveway. "Go on home," Joe whispered. "I'll get the message to the plant. I just hope I'm not too late."

Zoe scanned the sky in the direction of the bomber

plant, half expecting to see smoke or flames. A head-line flashed before her eyes:

CHILDREN TOO LATE TO SAVE PLANT
Courageous Efforts in Vain

"Go on!" Joe said, giving her a shove. "We'd better not get caught now." He turned and ran for home. Zoe grabbed Rosie and they ran in the other direction.

(19)

Zoe got into her pajamas, the only clean pair she had left. A moth was beating its wings against the window screen. She wondered whether Joe had called the bomber plant yet. What would happen if he had? Would there be sirens? Would somebody blow the noon whistle? What if they could tell that Joe wasn't a grownup and they didn't believe him? Zoe worried.

Her room was a wreck. She picked up her shorts and shirt from the floor and stuffed them under her mattress. She was beginning to think of it as a laundry bag.

She sat on the edge of her bed and thumbed through a *Photoplay*. There were a lot of pictures of Betty Grable at the Hollywood USO. That made her think of Bernice. She bet dancing with Bernice was a shock after Betty Grable.

She scratched her newest mosquito bites and decided to go to bed. If there was going to be an explosion, it would wake her up. Anyway, there was nothing she could do now. It was up to Joe. She stood up and pulled back the bedspread. She noticed that the mattress was getting humpy with dirty clothes.

"Zoe?" Rosie's voice was so soft Zoe almost didn't hear her.

"What do you want?"

"My doll!" Rosie's chin was shaking and her eyes were full of tears. "I lost her!"

"How?"

"I think she fell out of my pocket when we were at Miss Lavatier's."

"Under the porch?"

"I don't know. Maybe. Or maybe coming home. I had her when we were sitting under the bush."

"We can look for her in the morning."

"But if she's under the porch, we can't." Rosie's voice began to quaver. "We can only go under there at night!"

"Do you think she's under the porch?"

"I think so. My pocket ripped when we crawled through that little door."

"Going out?"

"Going *in!*" Rosie wailed.

"Oh."

"And I can't go to sleep," Rosie sobbed. "I can't even stop crying."

Tears began to roll down Rosie's cheeks and she let them. Something about seeing tears dripping off Rosie's chin made Zoe feel awful.

"Couldn't you sleep without her just this once?" Zoe said, but she knew perfectly well Rosie couldn't.

"I could try," Rosie sobbed. "But it makes me feel all nervous." She wiped her nose on the hem of her nightgown. Now she was trying not to cry. That made Zoe feel worse than when she was crying.

"All right," said Zoe, "I'll get her for you. You go to bed."

Rosie sniffed. She took a long shaky breath and padded out the door.

Didn't even say thank you, Zoe thought crossly. She sat and looked at her bare feet. How was she going to get the doll? "Well, I'll just go down and get it," she muttered. "I won't think about it. I'll just take my flashlight and go."

She found her flashlight in the bottom drawer of her dresser. She tested it to make sure Rosie hadn't worn out the batteries. She listened until she was sure both her father and mother were in the living room. Then she took her flashlight and started down the back stairs. "Don't think!" she told herself, tiptoeing down, leaning on the railing.

The second time you do something it's easier, she thought. She was down the stairs and out the back door in no time. The back-porch light was on, so she hurried to get into the dark of the yard. Just as she reached the Victory garden she saw somebody walking up the driveway. She dropped down among the tomato plants and watched. It was only Bernice. *That* was perfect timing, she thought. She waited until Bernice had gone in the back door and switched off the porch light. Then she dashed across the grass and ran all the way to Miss Lavatier's house without stopping.

There were lights on in the house and the truck was in the driveway. Zoe crouched down and ran to the side of the porch. She found the door to the crawl space easily. She slipped through the opening and pulled the door closed behind her, then switched on her flashlight and swept its beam back and forth across the dirt floor. She didn't see the doll. Darn Rosie, she thought, she probably didn't even drop it in here.

She flashed the light carefully along the sides of the crawl space and into the corners. Then she shone it along the wall of the house. She saw a door in the wall. That must be the coal chute Rosie was talking about, she thought. She remembered that Rosie said it didn't lock and that you could see right into the cellar. Zoe wondered what was in Miss Lavatier's cellar. She was tempted to open the coal chute door a little way and look in. Better not, she decided.

She turned and shone the flashlight along the ground behind her. The beam came to a small hump on the ground. The hump was Rosie's doll. "Oh, good!" Zoe whispered. "That's that." She picked up the doll and tucked it into the elastic waistband of her pajamas. She switched off the flashlight. There was enough light from outside to find her way to the crawl-space door.

She put the flashlight under her arm. She was about to push her way out into the driveway when she saw a thin band of light coming from around the edges of the coal chute door. Something made her want very badly to open the door a crack and peek in. She felt suddenly more curious than afraid. Joe Bunch would do it, she thought. He'd do it in a minute.

She crawled back to the coal chute. She hesitated. What if the door creaked or banged or something?

LOCAL GIRL FOUND SHOT
Body Discovered under Local Porch

That's the difference between me and Joe Bunch, Zoe thought. He never thinks about the bad things that could happen. That's the first thing I think about. I have a very depressing imagination.

She ran her finger around the edge of the door. It wasn't tightly closed. Carefully she wedged two fingers into the crack between the door and the wall and pulled gently. The door didn't budge. She pulled a little harder and it came open a crack. Another crack and Zoe thought she would be able to peek inside. She gave the door a small tug.

There was a light on in the cellar. Maybe Miss Lavatier had forgotten to turn it off. Maybe she planned to come back. As far as Zoe could see nobody was there now. Zoe squinted through the crack. On one wall were the usual cellar kinds of things: a shelf of Mason jars, a few light bulbs, a broken folding chair, and some green garden hose. There was a furnace almost directly under the coal chute and, next to it, an old hot-water heater.

Well, that's all pretty dull, she thought. Still, as long as she was there, she guessed she ought to open the door another tiny crack and see if she could see the opposite cellar wall. She shifted position and eased the

174

door open a little wider. From that angle she could see the other side of the cellar all right. A dressmaker's dummy, a yellow lampshade, a—Zoe caught her breath. Piled against the wall were the cardboard cartons!

"There they are!" she murmured. "They didn't take them to the bomber plant!" The cartons were stacked along the length of the wall. Zoe guessed there might be fifteen or twenty of them, plain brown and unmarked. She was so excited that for a minute she just stared at them. Joe's telephone call would be in time. They'd saved the bomber plant!

Then she began to think about it. How had they gotten so many cartons from the crawl space to the cellar in broad daylight? All at once Zoe knew how they'd done it. They'd lifted them right through the coal chute, of course. That was why she had heard voices under the porch today. They were moving the cartons. They were standing *right here* moving explosives. She shivered. All at once she was scared to death. What am I doing here? I must be *crazy!* she thought. Suddenly all she wanted was to get out of there fast.

She pushed at the coal chute door, trying to close it. It wouldn't move. She wrenched, but the rusty door resisted. She grunted and shoved again with all her strength. Suddenly the door came loose from its hinges. Zoe lurched forward, losing her balance. She stumbled and crashed into something hard. Suddenly she was falling. She was flat on her face. Garden tools clattered around her. The wheelbarrow! she thought. A rake grazed her arm. Then something heavy hit her head.

(20)

Zoe lay still, too startled to move. The tools seemed to clatter and bang for a long time. A big patch of light from the open coal chute shone on her. Her head hurt. I ought to get out of here, she thought slowly. But it was so peaceful on the ground. She shut her eyes and watched blue spots swim back and forth like water bugs under her eyelids.

Everything seemed to be moving slowly. She lifted her hand and watched it float down again like a cottonwood seed. Her feet seemed very far away. "I'm dazed," she thought. She remembered something hitting her head. That was it. She sat up slowly and rubbed the lump that was beginning to grow on her temple. I wonder if I have amnesia, she thought.

Suddenly somewhere a screen door banged. There were footsteps overhead. They crossed the porch quickly and clattered down the stairs. Then there were voices. "It came from under the porch! It must have!" It was Miss Lavatier's voice.

Zoe froze. This was it, all right. This time she really was going to be caught.

"Give me the light," a man's voice said. Outside the

crawl space somebody switched on a flashlight. Zoe jumped to her feet. Her head whirled. She looked wildly around the crawl space for someplace to hide. Under the overturned wheelbarrow? They'd look there first. There was no way out but the way she'd come in. Except! In a flash Zoe knew what she had to do. She scrambled through the coal chute door just as someone rattled open the lattice.

She landed hard on the cellar floor. Pain shot through her ankle. She bit her lip to keep from crying out. Above her in the crawl space she heard the man's voice. Quickly she scuttled into the narrow crack between the furnace and the wall. She squatted down and pressed herself tight against the concrete.

"Somebody's been here all right," the man said. "There's garden tools all over the place. Hey, look here! They ripped the door off the coal chute, Lil!"

Zoe held her ankle with both hands. She was too afraid to move, too afraid even to think.

"Don't see how they got out either. Hardly had time to get away."

Zoe's ankle throbbed. Her heart was pounding in her ears. "Don't let them find me," she prayed.

"Do you think someone might be in the cellar?" It was Miss Lavatier's voice. She sounded frightened.

"Better have a look. You stay here. I'll go around and check the cellar."

Zoe felt paralyzed. They were coming after her! Somehow she had to get away. She looked up at the gaping coal chute. It was too high to reach. Besides Miss Lavatier was guarding the crawl-space door. Zoe looked wildly around the cellar walls for a way to escape. The only way out was the cellar steps.

Zoe jumped up. Pain burned in her ankle. Above her she heard the front door bang. She lurched around the furnace and stumbled toward the cellar steps. I've got to make it! she thought. I've got to hurry.

She grabbed the stair rail. She hopped and dragged herself up the first steps. She heard footsteps coming toward her overhead. "Six more to climb, five more, four more, hurry!" She hopped on her good leg, gasping for breath. Footsteps came closer. "Two more to climb. Hurry!" With a final lunge she flung herself against the cellar door. I've still got time. Still a second or two! She grabbed the door handle and turned. She shoved at the door. It wouldn't open. The door was locked!

She couldn't believe it. It was her only chance. A sob shook her. She stared at the door stupidly. As she stared, the knob turned. A key rattled in the lock. With a gasp Zoe hurled herself down the cellar stairs.

She forgot her ankle. She forgot everything but hiding somehow. She dragged herself under the cellar stairs just as the door opened.

Heavy steps came down the stairs. "I heard you," the man's voice said. "I know you're down here somewhere."

Zoe held her breath. White summer shoes passed by a foot away. "I'll find you. You can't get away," said the man.

178

Zoe peered out around the stairs. She saw him walking toward the furnace, carrying a flashlight. He shone it behind the water heater, behind the furnace, into the corners, checking carefully. "No use hiding," he said. "I've got you sooner or later now."

Zoe watched as he turned and came toward the stairs. He was checking behind everything, moving slowly down the wall toward her. His light moved into the dark corners, under and around every object.

She could hear him breathing as he came closer. He was so close she could see nothing but his legs now. He knows I've seen the cartons. He'll never let me out of here alive, Zoe thought. She pressed herself against the wall and closed her eyes.

She heard a shuffling sound almost beside her, a muffled grunt. Then a bright light shone on her eyelids. The man whistled softly. "Well, what do you know?" he said. "Lillian! Lil! I've found the prowler!"

Zoe heard the rapid click of Miss Lavatier's high heels on the floor overhead. "Prowler?" Miss Lavatier sounded timid.

"Come on down," the man called. "We're not in much danger. It's the little girl who skinned her knee. Remember, I told you." Then he turned to Zoe. "What in the devil are you doing here?"

Zoe didn't answer. She didn't look up. She wondered what they'd do now, how much longer she had.

Miss Lavatier appeared behind the man. She peeped under the stairs. "Why it's Zoe!" she said. "It's one of

179

my pupils!" She sounded relieved. She was almost laughing. "What on earth are you doing here, Zoe?"

Zoe didn't look up. She didn't reply.

Miss Lavatier crawled in under the steps beside her. "What are you doing in my cellar?" she repeated. She didn't sound mad exactly. Mostly she sounded worried.

Zoe said nothing. There was nothing to say. She couldn't think of a reason in the world to be in Miss Lavatier's cellar. And she wasn't going to talk. They could torture her all they wanted, she wasn't going to tell them about the war work. Not a word. Not for anything.

"Answer me, dear," Miss Lavatier said.

Zoe shook her head.

"Bring her upstairs, Lillian. We'll get her to talk," said the man.

Miss Lavatier pulled Zoe gently from under the stairs. "Look at her head," she said. "Look at the lump." Zoe closed her eyes. She couldn't look at them and not answer. It embarrassed her.

"Take her up to the front room," the man said.

Miss Lavatier took Zoe's arm and pulled her to her feet. Zoe's ankle throbbed suddenly. She winced. "I don't understand," Miss Lavatier said. "She seems to be hurt."

Together Miss Lavatier and the man helped Zoe to the stairs, one on each side. "We've got to call her father right away," Miss Lavatier said. "She's limping, too."

"Let's think about that later," the man said. "First, I want to know what she was doing in the cellar."

"But the child's hurt!"

"She was in the cellar, Lillian."

Zoe felt panicky. Would Miss Lavatier really call her father or was it a trick? She couldn't tell. What she had to remember was that there were explosives right there in Miss Lavatier's cellar. She'd seen them. They knew she'd seen them. That was what she had to keep in mind.

They reached the top of the stairs. Zoe's ankle ached horribly. They helped her down a sort of back hall into the living room.

Miss Lavatier sat Zoe on a straight-backed chair. "All right, now, Zoe, explain this to us," she said. Zoe squeezed her eyes tight and didn't say a word.

"Maybe she's scared," said the man.

Zoe peeped out through her eyelashes. Miss Lavatier was sitting opposite her. She had on an orange dress. "Answer me, dear," she said.

"Let me try," said the man. He came over and squatted beside Zoe's chair.

"I'm going to get some ice for her head. That bump's turning purple," Miss Lavatier said.

Zoe could hear her rattling an ice tray in the kitchen. The man took Zoe's arm. "O.K.," he said, "you can go home. We'll call your Dad as soon as you tell us what you're doing here."

Zoe squeezed her lips tight. Would they really let her go if she told them? Of course not. Either way she'd never get home again. Her throat felt tight. She was trembling. If only I could think of a lie to tell them, she thought, but she was too afraid to think.

"Let's have it, kid. What were you doing down there?" The man had stopped sounding nice. His voice was rough. He tightened his hold on her arm.

Zoe closed her eyes.

"Here, let me put a little ice on your head." Miss Lavatier pressed a cold cloth against Zoe's temple. "Now I'm going to telephone her father," she said.

"Hold it, Lillian."

"No. I'm going to. For all we know she may have a concussion."

The man took Zoe's hand and pressed it against the cloth. "You hold that," he said. "Come here a minute, Lillian."

Zoe peeped through her eyelashes. The two of them had walked into the front hall. "What are they going to do now?" Zoe thought. "Is this when they start torturing me?" She held tight to the wet cloth against her temple as if it had a magic power to save her.

They were talking softly. "I want to call her father," Miss Lavatier said.

"How do we know what she saw down there?" the man whispered.

"What does it matter? She's only a child."

"So, a child's got eyes. It's damned strange to find her in the cellar at ten o'clock at night. You've got to admit that."

"Yes, but—"

"So what was she doing there?"

"I don't know, but certainly nothing to do with that."

"Yeah, but what if she mentions what she saw? You want the whole thing to blow up on us?"

There it was again! Blow up! Explosives! Zoe trembled.

"She's hurt. We have to call her family. A few cardboard cartons, after all—"

"Ssh!"

Zoe could hear Miss Lavatier murmuring something quietly. The man said something. Miss Lavatier murmured again. They know I saw the cartons. They know I know what's in them, Zoe thought. They're only pretending they might call my father.

All at once the man said, "All right, but I don't like it."

Zoe held tight to the cold, wet cloth.

"All right," said the man, so loudly that Zoe knew she was meant to hear, "but if that kid blabs anything about what's in your cellar she'll be sorry. I'll see to that."

"Hush," said Miss Lavatier. "Don't say that."

"I mean she'll be sorry," the man repeated.

Zoe closed her eyes and waited for what would happen next. What did the man mean, she'd be sorry? She held tight to the chair and waited. All at once she heard someone dialing a telephone.

Zoe sobbed. She couldn't help it. Maybe they really were calling her father! She bit the inside of her cheek to try to stop crying. Whatever happened now, she meant

184

to face it bravely. She wasn't going to be a blubbering baby at the very last minute.

She could hear Miss Lavatier's voice sounding polite. Then she heard the receiver rattle down and Miss Lavatier's high heels clicking across the front hall. "Your father is coming to get you," Miss Lavatier said.

Zoe still wasn't sure it was true. She sat up straight and kept her eyes closed. "I'm going, then," the man said. Zoe heard the front screen door open and Miss Lavatier saying something softly.

"If that kid blabs, she'll be sorry." Zoe remembered how his voice sounded saying that. Well, he doesn't have to worry, Zoe thought. I'll never say a thing. At least not until the FBI catches them and has them locked up.

But how did they know she wouldn't talk? For all they know I'll go right home and tell everything, she thought. How can they trust me? Zoe fingered the lump on her head. I wonder if it is a concussion, she thought. I wonder if I have brain damage. She didn't think so, but suddenly she had a wonderful idea. She would let *them* think so! A person with brain damage couldn't talk. If they thought she had brain damage they'd think she couldn't give away any secrets! Luckily she hadn't said a word since they'd caught her. It's got to work, she decided.

She heard the front door close and then the sound of Miss Lavatier's heels in the hall. "Your father should be here any minute," Miss Lavatier said. "I'm going to get some more ice for your head." Zoe pretended not to understand a word. She stared straight ahead and hoped she looked stunned. It was her only chance.

While Miss Lavatier was in the kitchen getting ice, the doorbell rang. In a minute Zoe heard her father's voice at the front door. "I have no idea," Miss Lavatier said.

"Terribly sorry," said Zoe's father.

Zoe was afraid her father would make her stay until she explained herself. It would be harder to act stunned in front of him.

He walked into the room and looked at her oddly. "She has a bump on her head," Miss Lavatier said, "and I'm afraid she may have sprained her ankle."

Zoe's father wiggled her ankle up and down. He looked at the lump on her temple. "Nothing serious," he said. "I'm awfully sorry she bothered you. I'll take her home now and I'll certainly find out what's been going on."

"Well, children are funny," Miss Lavatier said in a tea-party voice. "I'm just glad she isn't badly hurt."

All the way home Zoe was silent. Her father didn't say anything either. She limped along beside him. He held her arm. Her mother was standing on the front porch with Rosie, and Bernice was peering out the screen door. They all looked scared. "What on earth have you been doing?" her mother said.

Rosie was making a face at her. It's supposed to be some kind of message, Zoe thought.

"Well?" said her father.

Zoe didn't answer. She didn't dare. She couldn't trust her family not to tell Miss Lavatier she'd talked. Even if she explained her reasons carefully, they might think she was just being silly. They'd never believe what she had to tell them. They'd think she was just imagining things again. They might even call Miss Lavatier and tell her, as though it were a joke. The only thing to do was not to talk at all.

"Well?" her father said again. Zoe said nothing. They led her into the living room and sat her on the sofa. Rosie stared at her as though she'd just come back from Mars. "Will you look at the lump on her head!" said Bernice.

"Oh, her head's hurt, too!" her mother said. "Maybe she *can't* talk!"

"It's just a bump," said Zoe's father. "She can talk all right. She won't, is all."

Zoe wondered how he knew that. Somehow she had to convince him, too, that her brain was damaged.

Her mother sat beside her and stroked the lump on her temple. Zoe winced. She wished they would leave her alone. If she had a few minutes to think she might figure things out better.

Her father pulled a chair up to the sofa and sat down opposite her. "Now we'll have to have an explanation," he said. "You can't appear in Miss Lavatier's cellar in the middle of the night and not explain yourself."

Zoe closed her eyes. It really was easier not to talk if you weren't looking at anyone. She could understand how ostriches felt.

"Rosie, she has your doll!" their mother said.

"Yep." Zoe waited. Rosie was probably going to spill everything now.

"Why does she have your doll?"

"Sometimes I let her use it."

"I've never heard of that. I don't think you do." Zoe could tell from her mothers' voice that she was trying to be clever. This was the voice she used for worming information.

"On the Fourth of July I do," Rosie said, "for special."

"This is ridiculous," said their father. "Something's up and I want to know what it is."

"That's what I think," Bernice said. "Something fishy's going on."

"Well, I'm not going to stay up all night finding out," her father said. "Tomorrow we'll get to the bottom of this. Tonight we'll all just go to bed." He stood up. He looked grim. "Upstairs!" he said.

Zoe limped up the stairs after Rosie. Their mother started turning off lights in the living room. "Did they almost kill you?" Rosie whispered in the upstairs hall. Zoe pretended not to understand. She hadn't talked for so long that her throat felt rusted. Maybe she'd never be able to talk again. The more she thought about it, the more interesting that seemed.

"Thanks for getting my doll," Rosie whispered. "You can use her sometime maybe."

Zoe smiled. She was getting to like being a mute. It made her special. In a way it was like being very well co-ordinated or having naturally curly hair.

188

"I wish you'd talk," Rosie said. Zoe smiled again. She felt mysterious. If she forgot for a minute the reason she couldn't talk, she rather enjoyed it.

She limped into her room and got into bed. In a minute her father came in with an elastic bandage to wrap her ankle. "I don't know what all this foolishness is about," he muttered, pulling the bandage tight, "but I'm going to find out first thing tomorrow."

Zoe said nothing, not when he kissed her, not when he turned out the light. She could feel her heart beating in her ankle where the bandage squeezed. She was terribly tired. She didn't see how she could stop talking forever, but if the FBI didn't catch those spies, she'd have to. Maybe I'll never be able to speak again, she thought. For years I'll use hand signals. At least until I'm about sixty. She saw a headline:

FAMOUS MUTE AT LAST DIVULGES SECRET
World Awed by Story Old Woman Tells

I could call a press conference and tell all, after Miss Lavatier is dead, Zoe thought just as she was falling asleep.

(21)

Zoe was brushing her teeth. She almost never remembered to brush her teeth in the morning, but today she'd remembered because she didn't want to go downstairs. She could hear her father's voice in the breakfast room. That was a very bad sign. He never stayed home from work on Monday mornings. Of course, he was home today, Zoe knew, because he was going to question her.

She brushed her teeth with a circular motion, admiring the way her braces gleamed through the foam. They looked like buried treasure. Treasure made her think of diamonds. Diamonds made her think of Joe Bunch.

She could see why Joe kept a notebook. I ought to keep a notebook, she thought. I've got so many problems I can't keep them straight.

She took a mouthful of water and rinsed. Before her braces she had been able to squirt water between her front teeth. She missed doing that. A lot of things had been better in the old days. For one, she hadn't had any worries.

Being a mute didn't seem half as interesting as it had the night before. In fact, it seemed awful. How was she going to sit there and never say a word while her father questioned her? Well, she had to, that was all. The only person she dared talk to was Joe Bunch and she didn't see how she could do that. Joe couldn't leave his house and mutes couldn't use the telephone.

Maybe Rosie could take him a note, Zoe thought. Then she groaned. Rosie! Why hadn't she thought of that before? Of course Rosie had told everything by now. She was a terrible secret keeper even under perfect conditions. Zoe could imagine her sitting at the breakfast table explaining it all. She'd get it mixed up and wrong, naturally, so things would be worse than ever. Zoe put her toothbrush in the medicine cabinet. She closed the door. Might as well go down and face them, she thought.

She started slowly down the stairs. What if by some miracle Rosie hadn't talked? In a way Zoe almost hoped she had. That would settle things. But if she hasn't, Zoe thought, I'll just have to be mute. It's the only way. Maybe Daddy will really believe I have brain damage. Maybe they'll put me to bed and I can just stay there until the War's over.

That wouldn't be so bad, she thought. Bernice could bring her hot or cold lemonade, depending on the season. She could listen to all the soap operas on the radio and get pale. Doctors would come from New York to study the disease and write about her in medical journals:

CHILD SUFFERS RARE MALADY
International Conference Called

I'd have to have some new pajamas, Zoe thought.

Of course her father would more likely *not* believe she had brain damage. He was hard to fool. Maybe if I acted a little crazy, too, it would be better, she thought. She wondered how you acted crazy. She knew she'd have to figure it out fast because she was already in the downstairs hall.

The only crazy person she knew about was in *Jane Eyre*. Mr. Rochester's wife had been crazy. She'd burned the house down. That's too much, Zoe thought. Then she remembered a movie she'd seen. The heroine had gone crazy. She had wandered around in a sort of daze with her hair hanging in her face. If anyone talked to her, she'd smiled this weird smile and waved her hands around in circles.

Zoe looked at herself in the hall mirror. The lump on her temple was almost gone. Her ankle barely ached at all. She ruffled her hair. Some of it fell over her eyes. She tried looking dazed. This is going to be embarrassing, she thought.

Bernice was in the kitchen sterilizing Mason jars. Everyone else was still at the breakfast table. They were sitting looking serious, especially Rosie. In fact Rosie looked terrible. One glance and Zoe knew she hadn't talked. She could also see that nobody had forgotten last night. Well, here goes, she thought. She wandered into the breakfast room, trying to look as dazed as possible.

"Push back your hair, dear. It's hanging in your eyes," her mother said.

Zoe started to do it. Then she caught herself. She

stopped her hand halfway to her head and waved it in a circle. She hoped she'd done it properly.

"Good morning," said her father.

He thinks I'm waving! Zoe thought. What else can I do? She tried smiling in a dazed way.

"Feeling better?" said her father.

Zoe smiled. I can't just go on *smiling*, she thought. There must be other things brain-damaged people do.

Bernice came in with a bowl of cereal for her. "This is the last of this box, you'll be glad to know," she said. Zoe rolled her eyes.

"Good grief!" Bernice said. "You look daft!"

Well, Zoe thought, finally it's working!

"Eat your breakfast," her father said. "Then we'll have a little talk about last night."

Tics! Zoe thought suddenly. And twitches. That was something you did if your brain wasn't right. She twitched.

"Watch the milk!" her mother cried.

Bernice shook her head and went back to the kitchen. Zoe could hear her getting out the canning kettle. Then she heard the kitchen radio snap on.

"And in our local news," the announcer's voice said, "officials at the bomber plant report an unidentified telephone call last night—"

Zoe stopped eating and held her breath. Oh, boy, she thought. I'd forgotten all about that!

"—warning them of a sabotage attempt. The unidentified informant told of hidden explosives he believed destined for the plant."

"Did you hear that?" Bernice shouted.

"Rubbish!" Zoe's father said.

"Officials here believe the call may have been the work of pranksters," the announcer continued. "But security measures at the plant have been doubled and—" The telephone rang. Rosie shot out of her chair as though she'd been waiting for a chance.

"I'll answer," their father said.

When he came back he looked crosser than ever. "We all have to have new badges," he said. "Before I can go out to the clinic this morning I have to pick up a new security badge."

"Because of the explosive scare?" their mother said.

"Yes, the crazy idiots. I'd rather sit this War out on the front lines."

This was what their father said whenever the bomber plant changed a rule. Zoe took a bite of cereal and hoped he was leaving.

"I'll have to hurry," he said to her mother, "but I want you to find out about last night. I want Zoe to go down and apologize to Miss Lavatier this morning. After that we'll see what else." Zoe took a deep breath. She could handle her mother. Anyway, right now she had bigger worries than what her parents might do to her.

After her father left, the telephone began ringing. All her mother's friends wanted to discuss the bomber plant. "You stay here until I talk to you," her mother said.

Bernice was busy snapping beans. Zoe took the opportunity to fly out the front door. She wanted to go someplace to think. She had to get away while her mother was talking. She glanced in the direction of Miss Lavatier's house. Nothing was going on there. Zoe decided to go to the sumac patch.

She ran all the way to Victoria Street. She crossed Victoria Street and headed for the vacant lot.

It was a relief to be alone. "It's a terrible thing when you can't even think in your own house," she said out loud. It was the first time she'd used her voice and it surprised her. "Think," she repeated, then quickly glanced behind her to see if anyone had heard.

At the corner of Happy Hollow she stopped to watch a truck go by. There was a sign on the side that said, "Slap the Jap with Rubber Scrap." Why didn't Joe switch to rubber when he got tired of cans instead of getting us into this? she thought. It seemed years since Joe had made up the enemy agents. Really it had just been a week. Boy, a person's life can get wrecked in a short time, Zoe thought.

She crossed the vacant lot, wading in weeds. Burrs snagged at her bandage, but she kept going. The sumac patch was hot. She made her way to headquarters and flopped down on the pink blanket. "At least I have some privacy," she said. She planned to talk out loud to herself whenever it was safe, just to keep in practice.

There were three saltines left in the box. Zoe took one and chewed it slowly, lying on her stomach. She had to think, but she didn't want to. What she had to think about scared her.

The minute she'd heard the radio announcement she'd had an awful idea. They weren't the *only* people listening to War news. Everybody listened. Right that minute Miss Lavatier had probably been listening to the very same broadcast. "And," said Zoe, getting to the part that worried her, "she'll think I was the one who made the phone call."

Zoe took another bite of the saltine and rolled over on her back. "She'll have to think that. As far as she knows, I'm the only one who saw the cartons. She'll think I went right home and called the bomber plant last night. What else would she think?"

Zoe lay still and looked at the sumac branches overhead. All her silence had been for nothing. Even if she didn't speak for the next fifty years they'd never believe she hadn't talked now. That meant it was certain they'd take revenge. *She'll be sorry. I'll see to that.* The words glowed in her memory like a neon sign.

No place was safe now. They'd find a way to get her. She wondered what type of revenge they'd choose. With so many explosives to spare, she thought, chances are they'll blow me up. She hated to think of her father and mother and Rosie, even Bernice blowing up, too. It didn't seem fair. Still, the more she thought about it, the surer she was that they would blow up her house.

She closed her eyes and saw it happening, the roof flying off, the walls crumbling, her family's bodies shooting into the air. Next there'd be a fire. Zoe could see the furniture burning and all the jars of vegetables Bernice had canned that summer cooking on the shelves. She squeezed her eyes tight and tried not to see anything more. Her poor family!

MYSTERIOUS EXPLOSION DESTROYS FAMILY
Nothing Left

Except I won't even be alive to read the headline, she thought.

(22)

Usually when Zoe imagined tragedies she cried. It was a relief. Now her eyes weren't even wet. This was too serious. Miss Lavatier and that man really *were* going to get her. And they were going to do it with a bomb.

"I have to stop them," she said.

After that she lay still for a long time, thinking. It wasn't easy to stop people from doing something when you didn't know when they were going to do it. Zoe wondered how to save the family. It wasn't likely they'd move just because she told them to. And anyway, she couldn't talk.

Oh, yes, I can, Zoe thought wearily. I forgot. It doesn't make any difference now whether I talk or not. She sighed. It had seemed like such a good plan. But maybe it still *was* a good plan. If the enemy could be convinced that Zoe couldn't talk, they'd think someone else had made the phone call. Somehow she had to make Miss Lavatier believe she couldn't talk. But how?

She thought about sending Rosie over with the information. That was impossible. Rosie was not subtle. She'd walk up to Miss Lavatier and say, "Guess what?

My sister said to tell you she can't talk." Sending Rosie would just make things worse.

Zoe looked around headquarters, trying to think. Her eyes came to rest on the scissors and paste. She could send an anonymous note! Why not? Joe had left a few scraps of magazine behind. Zoe thought there would be enough letters for a short note.

She set to work at once, snipping letters from the scraps of paper she found. When she had clipped out a small pile she began trying to arrange words. There was nothing to glue the letters onto, she realized. They had used the only paper Joe brought for writing to the FBI. It made Zoe mad to think that she had gotten this far and couldn't get farther. "I'll use part of the saltine box," she said. "I don't care." She ripped the cover off the box and began pasting letters to the blank side. Lots of people eat saltines, she thought. They'll never trace the note that way.

She pasted quickly. She wanted to get the note to Miss Lavatier as soon as possible in case they were planning to blow her up today. How can I think things like that without fainting? she wondered. A week ago I couldn't have. War work must make you tough. She kept pasting. After about half an hour, she had a note which satisfied her. She read it over. It seemed all right.

TO WHOM IT MAY CONCERN:
Your pupil Zoe is a mute. She has not talked since she suffered brain damage at your house last night.

Zoe thought about signing it "Anonymous," but that didn't seem necessary. Besides, she was in a hurry.

She waved the cardboard back and forth in the air to dry the paste. Then she picked up the scraps and stuffed them in her pocket. The worst part would be leaving the note on Miss Lavatier's porch. But she had to.

She ran all the way to Victoria Street with the note under her shirt. It gave her stomach a strange square look.

I hope nobody sees me, she thought.

She stopped at the corner and checked the Bunches' yard. Joe's wagon was parked near the porch steps. Otherwise the yard was empty. In fact the whole street was empty. Zoe could see all the way to her house. Not a thing moved. Good, she thought. She walked right up the street, staring straight ahead. When she reached Miss Lavatier's house, she paused a minute to look around her. Then she darted up Miss Lavatier's sidewalk, dropped the note beside the front door, and flew back to the sidewalk, all without taking a breath.

If they want to blow me up, they never had a better chance, she thought. She was panting and her knees were wobbly, but she'd done it. She walked quickly toward her house. She didn't much want to go there, but she had no place else to go. Anyway, she was worn out.

She hoped she could sneak into the house without running into anyone. She crept up the porch steps and stood listening at the screen door. She could hear Bernice in the kitchen, nothing else. She opened the door cautiously and stepped into the front hall.

The living-room door was partly closed. Zoe could hear her mother's voice. She was talking to someone. Zoe tiptoed past the living room to the stairs. Maybe she was safe for a while. She was about to start up when she heard another voice. She stopped to see if she could recognize the visitor's voice. She could, all right! Her mother was talking to Miss Lavatier!

Zoe almost burst into tears. She ran upstairs two at a time and threw herself onto her bed. She was too late. Miss Lavatier had beaten her. The note, everything, was too late. "If only I'd thought of it sooner. If only I hadn't slept so long," Zoe moaned. But now nothing was any use. Miss Lavatier was sitting right in their living room. Probably she had the bomb in her purse.

Zoe knew exactly what Miss Lavatier would do. When her mother wasn't looking, Miss Lavatier would stuff the bomb under the sofa cushions. Then she'd make an excuse to leave quickly and be halfway down the block when the bomb exploded. Zoe wanted to scream to her mother to get out of the house. She wanted to yell. But it was hopeless. Her mother would tell her not to be rude to Miss Lavatier. In fact she'd make her come down and apologize. Zoe would be standing right there apologizing when the bomb went off.

At least Rosie would be safe. Zoe could see her from the window, playing with her doll out under the lilac bushes. "Well if she's going to be safe, I'm going to be safe, too," Zoe sobbed. "It isn't my fault if grownups never believe anything." She jumped up. Her knees were weak and her heart was pounding. "Good-by house. Good-by, Mother," she sobbed. She took a last look at her room and ran for the stairs.

That was when things began exploding. Just as Zoe started down the stairs there was a terrible bang. Then another and another and another. Zoe dropped to her knees. She covered her head with her arms. Not just *one* bomb, she thought. She brought lots of them! Again something banged. Glass crashed. Bernice began screaming. It sounded as though the whole kitchen were exploding. Zoe was paralyzed. I ought to run, she thought frantically. But she couldn't move.

Bernice came running into the front hall yelling. She was covered with blood! Zoe's mother flew through the living-room door. Miss Lavatier followed. They both looked terrified. From the kitchen came more explosions, more crashing glass.

"They're exploding all over the kitchen!" Bernice screamed. All three women ran toward the noise. "The tomatoes!" someone yelled. "Watch the tomatoes!"

Zoe couldn't imagine what they meant. Could Miss Lavatier have hidden the bombs in tomatoes? Now all three of them were shouting, "Look out!"

"Don't touch it!"

Zoe crept down the stairs. She was shaking all over. Her mother was screaming at Bernice. Bernice was screaming at her mother. Miss Lavatier kept saying, "Oh, dear! Oh, dear!" over and over again. The explosions had stopped.

Zoe tiptoed to the kitchen door and peeked in. Bernice

was standing in the middle of the worst mess Zoe'd ever seen. The kitchen floor was covered with canned tomatoes and broken glass. Tomatoes were hanging from the ceiling and running down the walls. Tiny bits of glass sparkled in the juice. Zoe could see that Bernice was not covered with blood after all. She was dripping tomatoes. Tomatoes were running down her apron. One large tomato lay in her hair.

"They just started exploding!" Bernice cried. "A whole week's canning!"

"Well, at least nobody was hurt," Zoe's mother said, but she didn't look happy.

"Tomatoes do that," said Miss Lavatier.

Maybe that was true. Zoe could see no way that Miss Lavatier could have gotten bombs into Bernice's canned tomatoes.

"What happened?" Rosie said. She had come up behind Zoe. She stood looking into the kitchen with wide eyes. Everyone turned around.

"Exploded!" Bernice shouted.

"Hush now, we'll all help," their mother said. She looked distracted. Then she noticed Zoe.

"Where have you been?" she cried. "Miss Lavatier came over to be sure you were all right. I want you to apologize to her right here and now."

But I can't, Zoe thought. If I say one word she'll know I'm not a mute. Then she'll read the note and know that it's a lie. Then she'll get worse revenge on me than ever.

"Right now!" her mother said.

Zoe just stood and stared at the kitchen floor. She felt miserable. "Zoe can't talk," Rosie said.

"Nonsense!" said their mother.

Zoe felt so awful she wanted to die. She wished all those explosions *had* been bombs. There just wasn't any way to make things right. No matter what she did, things kept turning out worse than ever.

"Please apologize at once," her mother said.

Zoe took a shivering breath that felt like a sob. She turned around and ran out of the room. She raced up the stairs and into her bedroom. She slammed the door, locked it, and fell onto her bed. Then she cried.

She cried for a long time and it made her feel better. She didn't know what had happened downstairs. She didn't care. She just wanted to stay locked in her room forever.

The wind whipped her bedroom curtains. There was a crash of thunder, and rain began spattering outside. Zoe blew her nose and looked out the window. It was going to be a real storm. Automatically she closed the window to keep the rain out. She stood watching the wind bend the treetops and flip the wet leaves silver-side up. She liked storms. Bad weather cheered her up. She sighed. She thought of one good thing about the mess she was in. She wouldn't have to take any more dancing lessons.

(23)

And she was right about that. Tuesday, Wednesday, Thursday, and Friday came and went. On Saturday morning nobody even mentioned dancing lessons. By then they were all too worried about her.

Of course, Zoe hadn't stayed locked in her room. In fact she had come downstairs for dinner that very night. Dinner had been late because of the tomatoes. By the time they called her she'd been too hungry to stay locked in. But she hadn't talked. And she didn't talk the next day or the next. In fact, nobody had heard her voice since the Fourth of July.

It was an awful strain at first, keeping quiet, but after a while it got to seeming normal. In the beginning her father was very mad. He planned to punish her. He shouted at her. He reasoned with her. Then he coaxed her and pleaded with her. He took her temperature and X rayed her skull. Finally, when nothing changed her mind, he just started looking worried. Her mother looked worried too. Zoe could tell that even Rosie had begun to worry about her.

Bernice stopped canning beans for one whole day and

baked a two-layer coconut cake just for Zoe. It was delicious. Zoe ate it all by herself. Doing that gave her a nice crabby feeling. I'm like Scrooge, she thought, selfish and glad of it.

Not talking, she had a lot of time to think, and she made a very important discovery. Nobody, she realized, could make her talk! They could threaten and scream and coax and plead, but if she didn't want to talk she didn't have to. She felt powerful. She liked feeling that way. The more worried her father looked, the more powerful she felt. It was like finding she had magic she'd never known about.

Sometimes she got tired of everyone looking worried. Once in a while even her new feeling of power got to be a bore. Then she walked to the sumac patch and lay on the pink blanket and talked out loud to herself. Sometimes she talked with a British accent, sometimes she tried to sound French. It was kind of a weird thing to do, she realized, but everything had gotten so weird it didn't matter. Nobody had ever been so polite to her before. Nobody had ever baked her a whole cake of her own. So why should she act normal?

She'd even begun to worry less. Five days had gone by since the Fourth of July. Surely if Miss Lavatier were planning to bomb her she'd have done it by now. Zoe reasoned that Miss Lavatier must have found the note and believed it. That was why nothing had happened. As long as she stayed mute, Zoe felt she was fairly safe.

She wished that somehow Miss Lavatier and her boyfriend would get caught so things could get back to normal. She was counting heavily on their letter to the FBI. One thing was certain, though. No matter what happened, *she* wasn't going to do anything more.

On Saturday moring Zoe lay on the pink blanket and practiced sounding Japanese. She wasn't any good at it. The blanket was damp and smelled of mildew, and Zoe was tired of talking to herself. The problem with talking to yourself was that finally you ran out of conversation. Well, it's better than being dead, she thought.

Joe Bunch was getting out of his house that day. His father had finally decided that Joe had learned his lesson. I hope he comes to headquarters, Zoe thought. She was dying to talk to Joe. Anyway, she hoped Joe would think of some way to speed up Miss Lavatier's capture. She'd spent a long time hanging around the corner of Victoria Street on her way to headquarters in case Joe was looking out a window. She hoped he'd seen her heading for the vacant lot.

She sat up and hugged her knees. She stared out through the sumac stalks. "Maybe if I close my eyes and count to five, when I open them I'll see Joe coming," she said. She shut her eyes and counted slowly. "Five," she said and opened them. She blinked. What she saw was not Joe Bunch. What she saw was Miss Lavatier's boyfriend walking toward the apple tree.

At first she thought he was coming for her. Maybe he'd seen her duck into the sumac. She crouched on the balls of her feet, ready to run. But the man walked straight to the apple tree. He took a piece of paper from his shirt pocket and dropped it into the hole. Zoe watched while he glanced quickly around him. Then he hurried away toward town, exactly as he had done before. "O.K." she said. "I'll get the note." She was hardly even nervous.

She walked calmly across the vacant lot to the apple tree. She shinnied up the trunk and peered down into the hole. The paper had caught on some bark along the side. It was simple to reach it. She tucked the note into her back pocket and swung herself down to the ground. The whole thing had taken less than five minutes. She walked leisurely back to headquarters. I don't know why we hurried so before, she thought. Mr. Pear won't be along for half an hour. She sat down on the blanket and unfolded the note.

The first thing she noticed was that Miss Lavatier's boyfriend had terrible penmanship. His writing was crooked and babyish. Rosie can write better than this, Zoe thought. Then she began to read the note. It was short, just a few words. It said: "10–12:01–6 Hold at Station Trouble."

Where's Station Trouble? Zoe wondered. It didn't matter. Whatever the note meant, it was definite evidence. It was the only real piece of proof they had. The paper had an enemy's writing on it. It probably had his fingerprints all over it, too. We should have kept the last note, Zoe thought. She wasn't putting *this* one back in the tree.

She wrapped the note carefully in a piece of waxed paper from the inside of the saltine box. She knew you had to be careful not to smudge fingerprints. She folded the waxed paper into a small packet and tucked it securely into her shorts pocket. She had no idea what she'd do with the note. She just wanted to be sure she had it for future emergencies.

It made her smile to think of fat Mr. Pear fumbling around inside the apple tree for the note. In a way she wanted to stay around and spy on him just to see the look on his face when he found the note was missing. She decided instead that she'd better go home. It was nearly noon and Bernice was making toasted-cheese sandwiches for lunch.

Going home, she went through alleys as much as she could to keep from running into Mr. Pear. She had forgotten how interesting alleys were. Seeing houses from behind was like seeing people in their underwear. I haven't seen many people in their underwear, Zoe thought, but the ones I have seen look completely different from when they're dressed.

Passing behind Miss Lavatier's house, Zoe thought about the note she'd written. She wondered whether something about writing the note had made her braver. Since the awful tomato afternoon nothing had really scared her much. She didn't know why. It didn't make sense. But she knew she was different.

Maybe partly it was her new powerful feeling. Finding out that nobody could make you do something you didn't want to do was important. That way you started knowing what you wanted to do. You could figure things out for yourself. You could take care of yourself.

She walked up behind her own house and into the yard. She stopped to inspect the Victory garden. Everything needed thinning. Besides that, the weeds were terrible. I'll do it this afternoon, she thought. Two weeks ago her father would have been mad because she'd let the garden get so sloppy. Now he didn't say a word about such things, and for some reason that made her think of them. She wondered if grownups felt this way all the time.

She walked in the back door and slammed it. Nobody scolded her any more. She could slam doors, spill milk, not make her bed—anything. In some ways it was wonderful. The trouble was she didn't much feel like doing those things any more.

Nobody was in the kitchen. She could see that Bernice had started lunch. Ten slices of bread were lying on the kitchen table, buttered, waiting to be sandwiches. Zoe took a slice.

No one was in the kitchen. They were all in the living room. Even Bernice. Zoe wondered what was going on. She crept through the dining room into the front hall and perched at the foot of the stairs, out of sight of the living-room door. She wanted to eavesdrop. They were probably talking about her, as usual.

Rosie was babbling about something. Then Zoe heard Joe Bunch's voice. She wondered what Joe was doing there. I suppose he's looking for me, she thought. Then she heard her father.

"Now let's just get this straight," he said.

I was right, Zoe thought, he's trying to find out about me again. She could tell by the tone of his voice.

"Well," said Rosie. "I got too worried. My stomach was aching and everything. So I went and got Joe."

Zoe took a big bite of bread and butter.

"Yes?" her father said.

"And I said we'd better tell you," said Joe.

Zoe took another big bite and chewed slowly. She couldn't believe what she heard next. There was Joe Bunch, sitting right in her living room, telling her father the whole story. First he told about the note in the apple tree and about seeing Miss Lavatier's boyfriend and Mr. Pear. Then he told about Mr. Bunch's slashed awning and Miss Lavatier's boyfriend threatening him. He told about Zoe's falling down, about the explosives under the porch, about the call to the bomber plant—everything! Zoe didn't know whether to be mad or not. Joe had a right to tell, she supposed. Still, after she'd about killed herself keeping it secret it didn't seem fair.

Her father kept saying "Yes" and "I see." Whenever Joe got to an exciting part her mother said, "Oh, dear" and Bernice made clicking noises.

"So," Joe said, "Rosie and I got worried about Zoe. That's why we decided to tell you all about this. I don't know what happened down at Miss Lavatier's that night, but it must have been something awful."

"Hmmm," Zoe's father said.

"Personally," Joe Bunch said, dropping his voice to a loud whisper, "I think she's been poisoned with nerve gas!" Zoe snorted. Nerve gas! She felt like laughing, but at the same time she felt like crying. Imagine Joe Bunch being worried enough about her to give away all his War secrets!

Her father was clearing his throat. Then he blew his nose. Those were signs that he didn't know what to say next. Finally he said, "Well, Joe, all these things you've told us are odd, certainly. I can see that they might seem suspicious. On the other hand, there may be a perfectly good explanation for all of them. There's nothing definite to suggest enemy spies or sabotage."

"But the explosives!" Joe said.

"You don't *know* they're explosives," Zoe's father said. "You just think so."

"But the note!"

"Well, there's no connection between the note you found and anything else is there? You say the note had some numbers on it. Can't make much of that."

"If I just hadn't lost my Spiral," Joe said, "I could show you the numbers and maybe you could figure them out."

Zoe was surprised. Joe'd lost his notebook? She thought he never let it out of his sight.

"And what about when Miss Lavatier's boyfriend threatened my father?" Joe said.

"That does sound strange, but, Joe, sometimes children overhear grownups talking and misinterpret what they hear."

"If I just had my Spiral," Joe said. "I wrote it all down in there."

"Zoe would remember," said Rosie, "except she can't talk."

"And what about when Zoe heard Miss Lavatier and that man talking about explosives?" Joe said.

Zoe scratched her knee. She knew what she had to do. She had an enemy note in her back pocket. She had an enemy handkerchief under her mattress. She could remember perfectly what the enemy agent had said to Mr. Bunch and what he had said to Miss Lavatier. She sighed. She was going to miss the powerful feeling, but in a way it would be nice to talk to people again. She stood up and smoothed out her shorts. She took the little waxed-paper packet from her back pocket.

"You see," her father was saying, "you can't accuse people of being spies unless you know you're right."

Sometimes a person had to do things just because they had to, even if it meant revenge and bombs. Zoe sighed. She felt very old. She cleared her throat and walked into the living room.

(24)

She walked in and dropped the note into her father's lap. Everyone stopped talking and stared at her. Her father picked up the folded waxed paper and looked at her. "What's this?" he said.

"An enemy note," Zoe answered.

"She talked!" Rosie shouted. "She can talk!"

"Lord love a duck!" Bernice exclaimed.

"Say something, Zoe! Say a jump-rope song!" Rosie cried.

Zoe felt silly. You'd think she'd invented electricity or something the way everyone was carrying on. The only person acting normal was her father. He was reading the note. "This came from that apple tree?" he said. Zoe nodded. He smoothed the note out on his knee and looked at it carefully. Zoe felt like telling him to be careful of the fingerprints. Instead she sat down on the floor beside him and traced a squiggle on the rug.

"You found it today?"

Zoe nodded again. "I saw Miss Lavatier's boyfriend put it in the tree."

"These numbers," her father said. "The 12:01 must be a time. Station might mean railroad station."

"The 12:01!" Joe shouted. "There's a train every day at 12:01!"

"Mr. Pear works at the train station," Rosie said. Of course everyone knew that.

"Maybe the most important thing though," Zoe said, "is I found where they're hiding the explosives." Her voice cracked. She half expected to be blown up that minute. Everybody stared at her. Joe Bunch's eyes were glittering.

"You found out that night?" her father said.

"That's what I saw in the cellar. They've got hundreds of boxes of explosives down there." Zoe paused. "Well, a dozen anyway."

"And you're sure they're explosives?"

Joe Bunch sputtered. Zoe shook her head.

"Well, that's the point," her father said. "We don't know. We can't just go accusing Miss Lavatier of hiding explosives, can we?"

"But her boyfriend acted so suspicious!" Zoe told her father about the man threatening her and about why she'd had to stay silent. "So don't you see why we think they've got explosives down there?"

"I see why you think something's fishy," her father said. "But, Zoe, the thing is, there isn't much we can do. It really is not our place to go poking into people's cellars and accusing them of things about which we have no proof."

Zoe sighed. She'd known all the time that that was what he'd say. There'd have to be a case of dynamite under his own chair before he'd take them seriously.

Lighted dynamite, probably. She was afraid he'd make her take the note back to the apple tree.

"But we're saving our country!" Joe said.

Her father began to say something. All at once there was a clattering on the front porch. Someone began ringing the doorbell and pounding on the screen door at the same time. Bernice jumped up and hurried into the hall to open the door. "Come in, sir," Zoe heard her say. She sounded startled.

Mr. Bunch came stamping into the living room. His face was red. He was waving a piece of paper. Behind him was a man Zoe had never seen before. "Where is he?" Mr. Bunch shouted. "Where's Joe?"

It was perfectly obvious where Joe was. He was sitting right on the living-room rug. He looked like he was going to throw up.

"What *is* this?" Mr. Bunch shouted. He threw the paper onto the floor. Zoe could see that it was their letter to the FBI.

"Now, Harry, calm down," Zoe's father said. He stood and offered Mr. Bunch his chair.

"Calm down! I'd like to know why I should calm down! Do you see that?" Mr. Bunch pointed to the letter on the floor.

Zoe's father looked puzzled. The strange man stepped forward and shook his hand. "Mr. Yale from the FBI," he said.

Zoe glanced at Joe. He looked terrible. She had no idea how Mr. Bunch had gotten into it, but if the FBI was here, everything was going to be all right.

"How do you do?" her father said.

"I can see you're puzzled," said Mr. Yale. "This letter came to our Bureau in Washington. We get lots of letters, but we try to check them all. This one had Mr. Bunch's return address on the envelope, so—"

Zoe gulped. She couldn't believe it. How could Joe have been so dumb? She looked at him. He looked so awful she wished she hadn't.

"Can you beat it!" Mr. Bunch screamed. "*My* return address!"

"So," Mr. Yale said, "Mr. Bunch thought that maybe his son had something to do with the letter."

"Thought! I knew he did!" Mr. Bunch yelled.

Zoe's father picked up the letter and read it. He asked Mr. Yale to sit down. Then he told Mr. Bunch to be quiet. Zoe thought for a minute that maybe Mr. Bunch was going to kill her father for saying that. He didn't. Her mother made room for Mr. Bunch on the sofa and he sat down.

"Now then," her father said. "This is all very interesting." Then he began to tell Mr. Yale the story Joe had just told him. He showed Mr. Yale the note from the apple tree. He made Zoe repeat her part, the conversation she'd heard on the Fourth of July, the cartons she had seen in the cellar. He even made her go get the handkerchief from under her mattress. Then he paused. Zoe realized he had left out the part about Mr. Bunch and the Queenie.

"Now, Harry, the interesting thing is that the children swear this man Zoe overheard is the same one they heard one day at the Queenie. They think they heard him threatening you."

Zoe looked from her father to Mr. Bunch. She thought her father was the bravest man in the world. Mr. Bunch's face had begun to fade. Now it began to get red again. "That so?" he said faintly.

"They think he had something to do with slashing your awning."

Mr. Bunch fingered the crease in his trousers. He looked uncomfortable. Zoe thought he even looked a little scared. "Well, they're right." He looked at Mr. Yale and sighed. "Might as well tell you about it," he said.

Zoe suddenly felt sad. She hoped Mr. Bunch didn't turn out to be an enemy agent, too. Maybe he was crabby and mean, but he *was* Joe's father.

"A while back," Mr. Bunch said, "this fellow came into my store. Never seen him before, but he seemed like a nice fellow. He said he had a way of getting some things I might need—rationed things, you know. Well, I should have known something was wrong. Maybe I did know." Mr. Bunch stared at the floor and shook his head. "I guess I did kind of suspect, but I didn't think much about it.

"Anyway, he started bringing me things every so often—silk stockings, rubber hot-water bottles, things like that. I sold them at the Queenie. Went like fire, of course, being's as they were rationed. Sometimes he threw in a box of bubble gum, the real kind the children like.

"Well, one day he came in and said he had lots of cartons of this stuff. He said he needed a place he could store them. He wanted to use the back room of the Queenie because of the alley and all."

Mr. Bunch stopped and glanced at Mr. Yale. He looked so worried that Zoe really wished she could help him.

"I knew right then what was up. I knew I was mixed up with the black market. So I said no, nothing doing. I said I didn't want any part of that business. That's when they slashed my awning." Mr. Bunch sighed.

"What the children heard, I guess, was after that. The fellow came back and told me that if I mentioned anything about their operation, they'd do something else. He said they'd smash my windows, maybe, or worse. I said I'd call the police, but I didn't dare. I was afraid of what those racketeers might do then."

Zoe felt so sorry for Mr. Bunch by now that she was almost in tears. She knew exactly how he felt. It was awful to know somebody was after you to get revenge.

"Never saw the fellow again," Mr. Bunch said. "He isn't from around here."

"He's from Plumville," Zoe said.

Everyone turned to look at her. "How do you know that?" her father said.

"It was on his truck. 'Graves' Nursery, Plumville.'"

Mr. Yale was making notes. "It sounds to me as if you kids have uncovered a black-market ring," he said. "Those cartons in Miss Lavatier's cellar must be the same ones this fellow was trying to store at the Queenie."

Zoe glanced at Joe. He looked disappointed. "You don't think it's spies?" he said.

"Doubt it," said Mr. Yale.

"Think of Lillian Lavatier being a gangster," Zoe's mother said.

Miss Lavatier/the racketeer, Zoe thought to herself. She could make it into a jump-rope rhyme.

"And with those beautiful awnings and all," Bernice said. "It's a pity."

"Well," Mr. Yale said, "the thing to do now is go down there and have a look at the cartons."

Zoe gulped. She didn't want to go anywhere near Miss Lavatier's house. "All of us?" she said.

"I think it would be helpful to have you kids identify the cartons," said Mr. Yale. "After all, you're the only ones who've seen them."

"I bet they aren't there," Joe Bunch said. "I bet they're on the way to the bomber plant with them."

Joe Bunch didn't change his mind easily. "Joe, they aren't full of explosives, remember? They're full of stockings and hot-water bottles and bubble gum," Zoe said. Suddenly she grinned. If the cartons weren't full of explosives, then Miss Lavatier wouldn't be worried about the telephone call and she wouldn't be trying to get revenge! Zoe was so relieved that she could actually feel the worry running out her fingers and toes like water going down a drain.

"I'd be glad to go with you, Mr. Yale," she said.

"Not me," said Mr. Bunch. "I'm not going anywhere. No, sir."

"I'll talk to you later, Mr. Bunch," said Mr. Yale. "Stay available."

"Bernice and I will sit with Mr. Bunch," Zoe's mother said. "The rest of you go on."

"Just the children," said Mr. Yale.

Zoe's father got a funny look on his face, but he didn't say a word.

"I better brush my hair," said Rosie.

"Do you think our soldiers stop to brush their hair—" Joe Bunch began, but Zoe could tell he didn't have his heart in it any more.

They followed Mr. Yale down the sidewalk single file. Rosie was first, then Zoe. Joe followed them, looking grumpy.

"It's O.K., Joe," Zoe whispered. "You can't help it that they aren't real enemy agents."

Joe was kicking a stone along in front of him. "Who cares about the black market?" he muttered. He gave the stone a good strong kick and sent it flying down the sidewalk. It came to rest on Miss Lavatier's porch step.

Good thing he didn't hit Mr. Yale with it, Zoe was thinking as they turned into Miss Lavatier's front walk.

(25)

Miss Lavatier answered the door in her peach silk dancing clothes. She must have just gotten home from class, thought Zoe. Miss Lavatier looked first at Mr. Yale and then peered around him at the children.

"Yes?" she said.

Zoe couldn't hear what Mr. Yale was saying. She was standing with Joe and Rosie on the bottom porch step and he was speaking quietly. She could see Miss Lavatier's face, though. It got funnier and funnier looking.

"There must be some mistake," Miss Lavatier said. "You know how children imagine things." She smiled a little when she said this, but it was the kind of smile someone smiles when you step on his foot in an elevator.

Mr. Yale kept talking. Miss Lavatier kept shaking her head. Every so often she said, "Oh, of course not," or "Why, that's ridiculous!" Zoe stood on one foot and then on the other. She couldn't see what there was to talk about. Why didn't Mr. Yale just walk in? He must have a gun.

Joe Bunch looked bored. Rosie wasn't even paying attention. She was pulling apart a leaf. Probably she doesn't understand, Zoe thought. She wondered when Rosie would start getting intelligent.

All at once Miss Lavatier cried, "Certainly not! It's out of the question!" She tried to shut the screen door right in Mr. Yale's face. Mr. Yale's hat fell off. He didn't even pick it up. He grabbed the handle of the screen door with both hands and pulled. Miss Lavatier held on.

"It's the law, Miss Lavatier, you have to let me in!" Mr. Yale was trying not to shout, but he was shouting anyway. Miss Lavatier kept shaking her head. She looked scared to death.

Mr. Yale gave the door another tug and pulled it open. Miss Lavatier came along with it. "Well, for heaven's sake then, come in," she said. Mr. Yale beckoned to Zoe to follow him.

Zoe nudged Joe. She wanted him to go first. She followed him onto the porch, holding Rosie's hand. "This is simply outrageous," Miss Lavatier said. "It should be obvious I'm not a criminal."

"Which way to the cellar?" said Mr. Yale. Miss Lavatier didn't answer. "Which way, Zoe?" he said.

Zoe wished he hadn't asked her. She glanced at Miss Lavatier. Miss Lavatier looked sick. "Down the hall," Zoe said. Nothing could possibly happen with Mr. Yale there, she knew. Still, she didn't look at Miss Lavatier again.

"This certainly is a pretty house, Miss Lavatier," said Rosie. "Green is about my favorite color next to navy blue."

Miss Lavatier didn't answer.

"Cellar door's locked," said Mr. Yale.

One thing about Miss Lavatier, she was an awful actress. "Locked?" she said. "For goodness sake." But her face looked so funny that anybody could tell she knew exactly where the key was.

"So I'll have to have the key," said Mr. Yale.

"Now isn't that strange," said Miss Lavatier. "I seem to have forgotten where I put it."

"No trouble there," Mr. Yale said. "I can just take the door off its hinges."

Miss Lavatier looked confused. Zoe felt sorry for her. I have to stop feeling sorry for people like this, she thought. It ruins everything.

Mr. Yale was beginning to pry loose one of the hinges with his pocket knife. "Never mind," said Miss Lavatier. She reached in the pocket of her peach silk blouse and pulled out the key. She handed it to Mr. Yale.

"Thank you," said Mr. Yale. He put his knife back in his pocket and unlocked the cellar door.

Mr. Yale went down the steps first. Zoe followed as closely as she could. It made her nervous to have Miss Lavatier behind her. How did Mr. Yale know that Miss Lavatier wouldn't do something? He didn't seem worried at all.

The cartons were still piled against the cellar wall. Zoe was relieved. Sometimes in the last few days she had begun to wonder whether she might have imagined the whole thing. She had heard of people having hallucinations after they'd been hit on the head. But there the cartons were, just as she'd remembered.

Maybe there weren't quite as *many* as she remembered. They weren't stacked to the ceiling. In fact, they weren't stacked as high as Mr. Yale's head. Still, there were a lot of them.

"These are the cartons?" Mr. Yale said.

Zoe nodded.

"Same ones you saw in the crawl space?" he asked.

"I think so," Zoe said.

"Replacements," Joe muttered under his breath. He wasn't giving up for anything, Zoe could see. In some ways Joe Bunch was very childish.

"Well, let's have a look." Mr. Yale got out his knife again. He picked up the nearest carton.

Miss Lavatier was standing on the bottom step watching. "I had nothing to do with this," she said. "I don't know anything about this." She sounded worried. "I asked them and asked them not to store things here."

Mr. Yale grunted. He slit the carton top with his knife. He folded back the top and looked into the carton. Zoe and Rosie stood on tiptoe and peered in, too. Inside were stockings, dozens and dozens of pairs of stockings, wrapped in white tissue paper. Mr. Yale grunted again.

"Stockings, Joe," Zoe whispered.

Joe Bunch was looking at the toe of his sneaker. He didn't answer.

"Well," said Mr. Yale, "this is very interesting. It looks like we have some black-market merchandise here." He picked up another carton and slit it open. Inside were more stockings.

The next carton was the same. Mr. Yale kept opening

cartons and muttering to himself. Zoe and Rosie and Joe kept standing there. It began to get boring.

Finally Mr. Yale turned to look at Miss Lavatier. "I think you'd better tell me all about this now," he said. He kept rummaging in the last carton he'd opened while he talked. All at once he stopped talking and stared into

it. Then he began tossing tissue-paper-wrapped stockings onto the cellar floor as if he'd gone crazy. Zoe wondered what he could be doing. Even Miss Lavatier looked surprised.

"What!" cried Mr. Yale. "*What* are *these?*" From the bottom of the carton he began to pull out small square

packages wrapped in brown paper. They looked like nothing but plain brown-paper packages to Zoe. She thought Mr. Yale must really have lost his mind.

He set each package carefully on the cellar floor. He put them down as though they were made of glass. Zoe looked at Mr. Yale. She looked at the packages. She stared at them, trying to see what Mr. Yale was so excited about. Each one was about the size of a box of bath powder. She crouched down and touched one curiously.

"Don't touch them! Stand back!" Mr. Yale shouted. Zoe jumped. She almost fell over. What in the world was the matter with Mr. Yale? She glanced at Joe Bunch. He looked excited, too.

"What are they?" she asked.

"Seen these things before," Mr. Yale said. "Saw the same kind of setup in San Francisco."

"But what *are* they?" Zoe repeated.

"Why they're explosives, girl!" Mr. Yale cried. "There's enough explosives here to blow up a small building."

(26)

Zoe couldn't believe it. She turned around and looked at the others. Joe Bunch was grinning from ear to ear.

"But how do you know?" she said.

Mr. Yale wasn't paying attention. He was feeling around inside another box. "If this is like the San Francisco job," he said, "there'll be about three cartons here half full of the stuff."

"I thought explosives looked like firecrackers," Rosie said. Zoe had thought that, too. She was glad she hadn't said so.

"Well, sir," Joe Bunch said, "it looks like we've got an enemy spy ring all right."

Mr. Yale didn't answer Joe. Zoe thought that was very rude of him. After all, if it hadn't been for Joe Bunch probably the whole town would have been blown up. Now that he was in charge of things Mr. Yale thought he could treat them all like children again. She felt like kicking him.

Mr. Yale straightened up and turned around. "Kids," he said, "this is serious business. Best thing would be for you to run on home now. I'll come around later and explain things to your folks."

"But, sir, we want to help you!" Joe said.

"Nothing you can do," said Mr. Yale. "I want to talk to Miss Lavatier here first thing. Then we'll see."

Zoe had almost forgotten Miss Lavatier. She turned to look at her. Miss Lavatier was sitting on the bottom step. She looked awful. "I don't know a thing about all this," she said. "The stockings, yes. Maybe I knew something about the stockings. But explosives! I swear I never knew there were explosives in there." Zoe didn't know why, but she believed Miss Lavatier. For one thing, nobody kept explosives in their cellar on purpose. Anybody'd have more sense than that.

"We'll see about that," said Mr. Yale. Zoe had a feeling he was about to tell the three of them to go home again when there was a lot of noise in the upstairs hall.

"Lillian!" somebody called.

Miss Lavatier jumped. She looked worse than ever. Mr. Yale stopped talking and stood with a bunch of stockings in either hand.

"Lillian!" the voice called again.

Zoe thought she recognized the voice. In another minute she was sure. Mr. Pear appeared at the top of the stairs. "Lillian," he said, "I've got the new shipment at the station but there wasn't a note. They didn't send the truck and—" Then he stopped. He had seen the rest of them standing in the cellar. "Why hello, children," he said.

"Come on down, John," said Miss Lavatier.

"This is very convenient," said Mr. Yale. "I thought we'd have to hunt you people up one by one."

Mr. Pear looked as wrinkled and fat as ever. Besides that, when he saw the stockings all over the floor, he looked scared. "John, this is Mr. Yale from the FBI," said Miss Lavatier. "He's found explosives in some of these cartons." Mr. Pear looked as surprised as Miss Lavatier. They really didn't know about the explosives. Zoe was sure of it. She felt sorry for both of them. Probably Mr. Yale would have them electrocuted or something. I wish I'd never seen these cartons, Zoe thought. I wish I'd just minded my own business in the first place.

She wondered if being electrocuted hurt much. Once she'd put a pair of scissors into an electric socket. That had felt terrible. "I don't think Miss Lavatier and Mr. Pear had anything to do with this," she said. She was surprised that she'd said it out loud. Joe Bunch looked at her as if he thought she was crazy.

"That's what I think, too," said Rosie.

Miss Lavatier made a kind of whimpering noise. "Of course we didn't know about this," she said.

Mr. Yale grunted. "Well somebody knew about it."

Miss Lavatier looked at Mr. Pear. He shook his head. Then her face just sort of collapsed. "Oh, no!" she said, "Oh, I can't believe he'd do it to us, John!"

Mr. Pear just stood there staring at the little brown-paper packages. His hands hung at his sides. "I think Mr. Pear and Miss Lavatier are innocent," Zoe said.

That reminded Mr. Yale that they were still there. "Now run along, kids," he said. "This is no place for children."

Joe Bunch argued a little, but it didn't do any good. Mr. Yale just kept shaking his head and saying they had to go home. "Come on, Joe," Zoe said. "Let's go."

"Good girl," said Mr. Yale. He started to pat her shoulder, but somehow it ended up that he was pushing her toward the stairs.

Really, Zoe was glad to go. She couldn't stand looking at Miss Lavatier and Mr. Pear, knowing they were going to be electrocuted, mostly because of her. She slipped past them on the stairs. She felt like apologizing, but she supposed that when you were about to be killed you didn't care if someone was sorry. When I get older I'll write a book about this, she thought. I'll put in all about how Miss Lavatier and Mr. Pear weren't really guilty. She hoped that would make her feel better.

In the upstairs hall Joe grabbed her arm. "Let's stand here and try to hear what they say," he whispered.

"Let's not."

"Why? What's the matter with you? You're acting nutty. First you say they aren't guilty. Then you don't want to listen. Why did you say that anyway?"

"That they didn't know about the explosives?"

"Yes, sure. You must be nuts."

"Because I don't think they did, Joe. I was watching their faces. They were as surprised as anyone."

"Well naturally they'd have to *act* surprised."

"No. They really were. You were the only person who wasn't surprised."

Joe Bunch smiled. "I knew it all along," he said.

232

"How?"

"I just knew. I guess I have a special kind of instinct for stuff like that."

Zoe sighed. One of the worst parts of this was going to be listening to Joe Bunch brag about his special instinct for the rest of the summer. Probably it wouldn't be just the summer, either. Probably he'd be writing compositions about it in school for the whole winter.

"Let's go home," she said. She took Rosie's hand and pulled her toward the door.

"I don't know why you're so funny all of a sudden," Joe said. Zoe pushed open the screen door. She wasn't going to answer him.

"Here we have a perfect chance to get more information and you won't."

"We don't need any more information. The FBI's running things now," she said.

Mr. Yale's hat was lying on the porch where it had fallen. Zoe looked at it. Probably she ought to pick it up and put it in the hall for him. Instead she kicked it. It flew up in the air and sailed over the porch railing onto the grass.

"Now what did you do that for?" Joe said. "You really must be nuts."

Zoe didn't answer him. She walked down the porch steps. She walked down the sidewalk. She stopped to hitch up her shorts, then she headed for home. Rosie trotted beside her. "Do you think Mr. Yale is torturing them?" she asked.

"No. That's not how they do it."

"I bet it is," Rosie said. "I bet he's going to torture them with bullets and knives and everything."

"Oh, Rosie, just shut up!" Zoe yelled.

"See, she's gone nutty," Joe said.

"You shut up, too!" Zoe screamed. She started to run. She couldn't stand either one of them. Fang came galloping along beside her. "You go home!" she yelled. "You dumb dog! Get out of my way!"

Right away she felt awful for screaming at Fang. Dogs didn't know anything. Even Rosie didn't know much. But she couldn't help it. She felt so awful she had to yell. And the worst part is I won't feel any better, she thought as her sneakers slapped on the sidewalk. Not ever. Not until I'm about eighty-five and my memory fails. She ran faster. She was almost home. Right then all she wanted was never to think about any of it again.

(27)

"Guess what! Miss Lavatier's house is all full of dyna-mite!" Rosie yelled. The front door slammed. Zoe was in her bedroom. She could hear Bernice come clattering out of the kitchen. She could hear her father and then her mother saying, "What!" She sat on her bed and felt awful.

"Joe Bunch says they'll get killed by a firing squad," Rosie shouted.

Zoe shivered. She heard everyone go into the living room. She had sneaked into the house and up to her room without being seen. In a minute someone would probably come after her. I'm a murderer, she thought. If it wasn't for me those people would live.

She stared at her shoe laces. What she felt like doing was curling up in a ball and lying under her bed. I haven't felt like that for ages, she thought. Not since I threw up on my desk in the third grade.

If she did that now she wouldn't even care. A person can't help something like that, she thought. It's the things you do that you *can* help! I didn't have to do this! I could have said "no" to Joe Bunch at the very beginning. But, no! I had to let him talk me into it.

And now here I am, practically a murderer! She could barely stand to think about it. "I wish I'd get amnesia," she muttered. "Not the kind where I'd forget my multiplication tables and all. Just the kind where I'd forget this summer."

She bent over and hugged her knees. Her head ached. Her stomach ached. Maybe I'll just die, she thought. She wondered how much you had to worry to die of it. She remembered her father had told her once about how people worried so much in the Depression that they died. Of course, a lot of them jumped off buildings. I'd never have the nerve, she thought.

"Where's Zoe?" she heard her father say.

She couldn't stand to talk to him. She scrambled off her bed and crawled underneath it. She lay on her back and stared at the bottom of the box spring. It was like a shallow cave under there. She was too big to curl up. She had to lie flat. Still, it was comfortable.

"Zoe?" her father called.

She lay still and held her breath. She saw the tag dangling from the mattress above the box spring. She gave it a yank and pulled it off. For a minute that made her feel brave. She almost laughed. The tag said "Do Not Remove Under Penalty of Law." For years she had thought that if she pulled it off a policeman would knock on the front door and arrest her.

GIRL ARRESTED FOR FOUL CRIME
Removes Mattress Tag
Held for Questioning

Boy, was I dumb in those days, she thought.

"Zoe?" Her father was right in the room. She hadn't heard him coming upstairs. "Zoe, are you in here?" She lay perfectly still. In a minute he'd go away.

She heard him open the door of her closet and rattle the hangers. She heard him walk over to the bed. All at once the bedspread moved and her father's face was peering at her. He looked puffy and funny upside down.

"Honey, what are you doing under there?" he said.

"Nothing." It was kind of a dumb thing to say, she realized, but it was the truth.

"Well, crawl out."

"Nope."

"Come on out and tell me what's wrong."

She hadn't meant to start crying. In fact she had planned definitely not to, but suddenly she was. She started with a big sob and then she couldn't stop. Her father knelt down beside the bed and tugged her out. He was bright red from bending over. He picked her up and held her on his lap. Zoe was surprised he could still lift her. She'd thought that she was too big.

"Now tell me," he said.

She couldn't. She didn't have breath enough for both talking and crying. He rocked her back and forth and let her cry. He wasn't as good at it as her mother, but at least he knew enough not to talk. Zoe cried for quite a while. It felt wonderful.

Her mother and Rosie peeked in the door and went away. Bernice came thumping upstairs saying something loud. Zoe's father shook his head and Bernice went away.

Pretty soon her mother came back with a wet washcloth to put on her eyes. That meant that it was time to stop. Zoe held the washcloth and took three or four gasping breaths.

"Now tell me," her father said.

"Well, to start with, I'm a murderer," Zoe said and started sobbing again.

"I doubt it," said her father. "Why do you think so?"

So she told him all about Mr. Pear and Miss Lavatier and the explosives Mr. Yale had found in the cellar. It was all her fault that Mr. Yale had found them, she said. And now Mr. Pear and Miss Lavatier would be electrocuted. And that made her a murderer. "Practically," she said. "Doesn't it?"

"No," her father said. "Absolutely not."

"Sort of?"

"No. If all this is true, if Miss Lavatier and Mr. Pear did know about the explosives, it's still unlikely they'd be electrocuted. And even if they were, it wouldn't be your fault, you know." He rocked her slowly.

"But I didn't have to spy on them! I didn't have to do any of that! They were *nice* to me. Mr. Pear gave us bubble gum. Miss Lavatier said she'd help me with my dancing. She even came up to see if I was hurt after she caught me in her cellar. Her boyfriend bandaged up my knee. Oh, Daddy, they were *nice* to us!"

Her father rocked her, nodding slowly.

"I didn't even want to do war work. I kept trying to

238

quit. I just did it to please Joe Bunch." Zoe sniffed. "No, that's not true," she said. "I did most of the worst part all on my own. Even after Joe was locked up I kept snooping. I was really proud of myself for doing it alone. Isn't that dumb?"

Her father just kept nodding and rocking.

"I thought I was doing something great. Very important. And now it's all my fault and they're going to get killed."

"Zoe, I told you I doubted that they'd be killed, so forget that. What you might think about instead is how many lives you saved. Supposing those explosives had gone off somewhere? Lots of people might have been hurt. Maybe you *saved* Miss Lavatier's life. Supposing those explosives had gone off in her cellar."

Zoe blew her nose. "You have to have a match," she said.

Her father smiled and rocked her gently. "You know, you're mixed up about some things," he said. "There's nothing wrong with being proud of doing things on your own. But you have to think about the consequences. If you jump into a mud puddle, you'd better plan to get muddy."

"Yeah, but you aren't hurting the mud any."

"So you have to think harder when it's people's business you're jumping into. That's all."

Zoe was beginning to feel better. She wished her father would stop talking now.

"Anyway, let's wait and see what Mr. Yale says. Maybe

we'll find that Miss Lavatier and Mr. Pear didn't know anything about the explosives."

Zoe nodded. "I hope so," she said.

Her father stopped rocking and sat her up. "Come on downstairs and have some lemonade."

Zoe didn't want to go downstairs with red eyes in case Joe Bunch was still around. She went into the bathroom and sloshed cold water in her face and thought things over. Probably her father was right. At least she wouldn't worry any more until Mr. Yale told them all about it. "A person can only stand just so much worrying," she said.

Mr. Yale didn't arrive until after dark and by then Rosie and Zoe were in bed. Zoe heard the doorbell ring as she was falling asleep. That's Mr. Yale, she thought. I'd better get up. She meant to get up. Lying in bed she thought how she would push back the covers, put her feet on the floor, and walk across her room. She thought how her door handle turned left but not right and how her bedroom door stuck a little bit. She thought about sitting at the top of the stairs and tracing figure 8s on the banister spokes while she listened to Mr. Yale and her parents. But somehow while she was thinking about it she fell asleep.

(28)

When Zoe woke in the morning she was furious. How had she possibly fallen asleep at such an important moment? She jumped out of bed and ran down to the kitchen. Bernice was squeezing orange juice. Nobody else was up. "What did he say, Bernice?" she asked.

"Who say?" Bernice was in her usual terrible morning mood.

"Mr. Yale! Didn't you listen last night when he was here?"

"Sit down and I'll get you some code cereal. You've only got half a box left."

"Didn't you hear?" Zoe repeated. She wondered if Bernice was trying to drive her crazy on purpose. She felt like kicking her.

"I did *not* hear. I don't eavesdrop," Bernice said. "I went upstairs after dinner. They had a special program on from the Avalon Ballroom."

"Oh, wonderful, Bernice," Zoe said. "Here we are in the middle of the most important thing that ever happened in this town and all you care about is the Avalon

Ballroom!" She scooped up a big spoonful of cereal and glared at Bernice. "You can throw out the rest of the cereal," she said. "I don't want a code ring." Who needed a make-believe code ring.

Bernice grunted. Zoe realized she wasn't paying any attention. "You can ask your father," she said. "He'll be down pretty soon."

Zoe finished her cereal, had a piece of toast, and worked half a crossword puzzle before her father came downstairs. He smiled when he saw her. "Good morning, Tokyo Rose," he said.

"What?"

"Nothing. I'm teasing you."

"But what does it mean?" Zoe's eyes widened.

"What? Oh, Tokyo Rose, you mean?" Her father laughed. "Tokyo Rose is a lady who broadcasts to our soldiers overseas. She's a kind of spy in a way. I was just being silly."

"But Mr. Yale was here?"

"Yup."

"So tell me!"

"She's been about to jump out of her skin," Bernice muttered. She poured a cup of coffee for Zoe's father. He took a cautious sip and put his cup down.

"Well," he said, "it's very interesting. Number one: you were right about Miss Lavatier and Mr. Pear. They didn't know about the explosives. They thought they were involved in a black-market operation, all right, but that's all. Mr. Pear took cartons off certain trains that came through here. He stored them in the baggage room at the station."

"At the USO!" Bernice murmured.

"I guess so. Right next to it anyway."

"That's a crime," said Bernice.

"Well, so, Miss Lavatier's boyfriend picked the cartons up at the station and took them to Miss Lavatier's. A fellow named Graves had a truck that they used."

"Graves' Nursery—Plumville," Zoe said.

"Right. They borrowed the Graves Nursery truck to move the cartons. Miss Lavatier's boyfriend had a room in Plumville. I guess so that he wouldn't be seen much in town. They stored the cartons in Miss Lavatier's cellar. You know that."

Zoe grinned.

"Miss Lavatier didn't like it much, I guess. She kept trying to get them to store the stuff someplace else, but her boyfriend persuaded her to use the cellar."

"That was dumb of her," Zoe said. "She should have known he was a gangster. Joe Bunch knew that a long time ago."

"Love is blind," said her father.

"That's the truth," said Bernice.

"I suppose Miss Lavatier never had many beaux," her father said. "She isn't very pretty. And it's a funny thing about ladies, you know. They'll do just about anything to please someone they love."

Zoe had a feeling that was true.

"Well, Miss Lavatier and Mr. Pear both knew they

were dealing in black-market goods. It scared them, too. One or the other of them was always wanting out. I guess Miss Lavatier did it for love, but Mr. Pear got paid a share of the profits for helping, so he kept at it.

"Mr. Pear took his share in goods. He sold stockings at the USO apparently. That right, Bernice?"

"I wouldn't know," Bernice said primly.

"One time Mr. Pear gave Rosie some bubble gum," said Zoe. "We thought it was poisoned."

"Not poisoned," her father said, "but probably black market. Did you chew it?"

Zoe shook her head.

"I gave it to Opal Wheeler!" Rosie said proudly. She was standing in the breakfast-room door in her pajamas. "I thought it would kill her."

"That's nice," said their father.

"You offered it to me first," Zoe said crossly. It irritated her that Rosie was up. Now she'd never get the rest of the story straight. "Go on telling me," she said. "Rosie, you be quiet."

"As you know, Miss Lavatier's boyfriend threatened Mr. Bunch once. Mr. Bunch didn't know him because he's not from town. He's the same man who bandaged your knee, right?" Zoe nodded. "Which reminds me to look at your knee sometime."

Zoe winced. "But tell me about the explosives, though. You never got to that part," she said.

"Oh. Well, Miss Lavatier's boyfriend knew about the explosives. He was the only one. He met Miss Lavatier in Chicago years ago. It turns out he is hooked up with a kind of enemy spy ring, but she never knew it.

"When the bomber plant was built here he remembered Miss Lavatier. He thought it would be easy to organize a group in town to receive black-market goods if she helped him. The explosives would be hidden here and there in certain marked cartons, but nobody in the group needed to know that."

"Then he *was* planning to blow up the bomber plant?" Zoe said.

"Looks that way. Of course, he won't admit it. Mr. Yale has him in custody and maybe he'll finally get it out of him."

"What's going to happen to all of them?" Zoe asked.

"I don't know for sure. But you don't have to worry about Miss Lavatier and Mr. Pear being electrocuted. They won't be."

"Or Miss Lavatier's boyfriend?"

"Doubt it."

"And Mr. Yale didn't torture them?" Rosie asked.

"Not that I know of."

"That was the part I was looking forward to," Rosie said. "Joe Bunch promised."

Zoe noticed that when Rosie said something especially stupid their father just ignored it. *I'll* try that, she thought. She might as well. Nothing else worked.

After breakfast Zoe went upstairs and made her bed. She pulled all the dirty clothes out from under her mattress and put them down the clothes chute. There was no reason to hide them any longer. The pajamas she'd worn to Miss Lavatier's the first time were beginning to mildew. And they were my best, she thought sadly. Maybe Bernice knows how to get out mildew.

Zoe felt funny. It was as though something important were missing. She tried to think what it could be that bothered her. While she thought about it she cleaned up the rest of her room. There was nothing else to do.

When she finished picking up Monopoly money and half-eaten cookies and the pieces of the Parcheesi game she sat down on her bed and wondered why she felt so strange. Was she still worrying about Miss Lavatier? She didn't think so. "I wish I had minded my own business," she thought, "but it's not my fault Miss Lavatier's in trouble. Not really."

Was it her new powerful feeling she was missing? Again she didn't think so. She could still *feel* it. It didn't seem to have much to do with being a mute after all. It had to do with being suddenly more grown-up, something like that. It was so new she hadn't got it straight quite yet.

"Then why do I feel so funny?" she said.

She looked at the scab on her knee. She remembered that her father wanted to have a look at it. Immediately she felt better. That was the trouble, she thought happily. I didn't have anything to worry about! Now she could worry all day about her father poking at the scab.

She bounced up and ran into the hall. She slid down the banister and banged the newel post. She went out the front door and stood on the porch, rubbing the place she'd just bumped. She shaded her eyes and looked in the direction of Victoria Street. Joe Bunch was just rounding the corner. Fang trotted beside him. Joe was pulling his wagon.

Zoe sat down on the steps and waited for Joe. It was going to be a very hot day. Maybe the hottest day of the summer. She picked a leaf and pressed it on her scab and watched Joe coming up her sidewalk. His wagon was full of flattened tin cans.

"Got any cans?" he said.

"Can't you rest from the war effort for one day?" she asked.

"Nothing more to do about the spy ring," he said. "You hear about it?"

"My father told me."

"Mr. Yale came down to our house, too. He told us all about it."

"Were you up?"

"Well, no. I heard about it this morning."

Zoe grinned. She knew it hurt Joe Bunch's pride to admit he'd been in bed.

"You were right about Miss Lavatier and all," he said.

Zoe nodded.

"I don't see how you knew that, Zoe."

Really it was very nice of Joe Bunch to admit she'd been right, especially when he'd been wrong. What she ought to do, she knew, was to let it drop. Instead, she shrugged casually and said, "I guess I just have a kind

247

of instinct for things like that, Joe." Joe Bunch frowned.

"Oh, hey! Look what I found. I almost forgot." Joe rummaged in his wagon. He held up the top of a saltine box. "It's got your name pasted on it," he said.

"Where did you find that?"

"Sticking out of a bush down the street."

Zoe took the box top from him. It was curled and rain-soaked. Most of the words she'd glued on were missing, but the words Zoe and *may concern* still clung to the cardboard.

"Isn't that weird?" said Joe.

"Yes," Zoe replied. She didn't feel like explaining things right then. Miss Lavatier must never have seen the note, she thought. It must have blown off her porch before she ever had a chance to read it.

"I'm going to the armory," Joe said. Zoe nodded. She watched him pulling the wagon until he was out of sight. Then she ran in to ask if she and Rosie could go swimming.

Late in the afternoon Zoe and Rosie were sitting on the front porch drying their hair. Joe Bunch was sitting beside them adding tin foil to his tin-foil ball. Fang lay on the sidewalk sleeping.

"Tomorrow we have to clean up headquarters," Joe said.

"I forgot to ask about the hole in the apple tree," said Zoe.

"I didn't," Joe said. "It was just like we thought. That gangster left notes there for Mr. Pear. That's how he told him when cartons were coming in. The numbers were the dates and the times of the trains and how many cartons to expect."

"What a dumb place to leave important messages," Zoe said.

"Mr. Pear had to go there on the way to work. They thought it would look natural if he stopped for a minute, I guess."

"I smell something terrible cooking," Rosie said.

"Catfish," said Zoe. "Daddy loves it."

If Bernice was cooking the catfish, it must be nearly time for dinner. That meant their father would be home any minute. Zoe clapped her hand to her knee and looked down the street. Sure enough, her father's Packard was chugging around the corner.

They watched him come up the street and turn into the driveway. "I'd better go home," Joe Bunch said. He stood up and hoisted his tin-foil ball into his wagon.

"Wait a minute, Joe," their father called. He jumped out of the car, waving a paper. "I've got something here you'll want to see." He handed the paper to Joe.

"My gosh!" said Joe Bunch. "Oh, my gosh!"

Zoe grabbed the paper out of his hands. She looked and couldn't believe what she saw. Right there in the evening newspaper in great big headline type she saw:

CHILDREN HELP CRACK ENEMY PLOT

"They mean us!" she said. She felt like crying.

"Let me see!" Rosie grabbed the paper and Zoe let

her have it. All of a sudden she didn't feel nasty or
crabby or worried or anything. What she felt was famous.
She wasn't used to it.

"I'll have to think this over," she said to herself. She
sat down on the porch steps and started to think.

ABOUT THE AUTHOR

Zibby Oneal was born and grew up in Omaha, Nebraska. She and her sister were eight and ten in 1944, during World War II, and they engaged in every patriotic practice recommended by the government or anyone else. "Those years still fascinate me. Looking back, they seem almost surrealistic. It was as though the whole civilian population in America had gone a little mad. Life was zany. As children, we were thrilled by the excitement of it all. We saw no moral issue. Children are different now. I try to explain how things were then to my own children and realize none of it makes sense to them. How could anyone ever have believed in war? The children are amazed. They're right to be amazed, of course. Still, that's how it was twenty-five years ago for their parents and it seems to me that the difference is worth remarking."

Mrs. Oneal, her husband, who is a plastic surgeon, and their two children, live in Ann Arbor, Michigan.